AI

Michael Stokes

Copyright © by: Michael Stokes.
apostlescreedms@gmail.com

ISBN: 9781091753914

Library of Congress: TXu 2-137-554

Acknowledgments

Special thanks to Jesus Christ. He set me free October 5th of 1997. For I can surely attest to this verse,

"not by works of righteousness which we have done, but according to His mercy He saved us, through the washing of regeneration and renewing of the Holy Spirit."

Titus 3:5

Thank you to my son Joshua Stokes who has always encouraged me greatly through this publishing process. Thank you, Joshua Stokes, for always being a light for our Lord & Savior Jesus Christ. I love you more than words can say.

M.A.P (Marketing & Publishing) group, thank you for all the help, and to Cathy Chapman, Author of "Redeem Region versus Strife State" Who placed countless hours editing for me.

Please read an especially
important note from the author
at end of book.

Table of Contents

1   The Big Night Out..............................1

2   Johnies Departure............................29

3   A Light in the Darkness....................49

4   Freedom From the Chains.................73

5   Spiritual Gifts..................................95

6   The Wilderness...............................119

7   Graduation from School of the Prophets......143

8   Revival Fire Spreads............ 161

9   Seeking to Save the Lost......... 179

10 Persecution Begins...............................195

Chapter One
The Big Night Out

Johnnie is shaken to his core as this large creature grasps him tightly with its razor-sharp claws. Not even knowing why he is in this cave filled with fire, thick yellow smoke while being attacked by this violent creature.

Instantly he is awakened with his 80-pound Labrador named Scout abruptly jumping on his bed. With his tail wagging, pulling the covers from his face, ears propped up, staring at him intently in hopes that Johnnie will pay him some attention. Pouncing up and down licking his face while unknowingly scratching him with his nails. Johnnie knows there is no escaping this playful attack. Thankful to be awakened out of this horrendous nightmare. He realizes that it is time to get up to meet the day.

He then notices the familiar scent of his mom's breakfast lingering in the air. Which usually consisted of eggs, toast, and of course some fruit for her son whom she loved. Johnnie had been enjoying this scent for all of his 18 years. Johnnie's mom always kept them strictly on a healthy diet.

As Johnnie was enjoying breakfast with his mom at the kitchen table. He was eagerly waiting for his best friend Mark to pick him up for school in his new Mustang GT that was all tricked out. They were both good kids excited to tackle the world, confident about their bright future.

Johnnie and his mom heard the loud deep roar of Mark's pipes shooting out of the back of his Mustang as he pulled into the driveway. Mark was also excited about the day, and of course his new set of wheels. So he arrived a little earlier than usual. Mark's stepfather bought him the car for getting the high honor roll and receiving a scholarship into UCLA's science program.

Since Mark arrived early to pick up Johnnie, he was forced to eat a nutritious breakfast with Johnnie and his mom Janice.

Johnnie was quietly feeling bummed out because he missed high honor roll. So, he did his best to be happy for Mark and celebrate with him. Johnnie had not yet found what his career is going to look like since he did not get accepted into UCLA. He was now forced to investigate a community college.

Johnnie and Mark hurried and shoveled down their food. They were anxious to take the new set of wheels for a cruise with their ladies who were the finest looking seniors at Ridgemont High School.

Johnnie was dating Priscilla, while Mark was seeing Rebecca. After checking out what the new Mustang GT could do on the Santa Monica freeway. Hitting speeds of one hundred and twenty miles per hour, yelling out the windows like a couple of crazed teens in the warm California early morning weather. They figured they better pick up the girls and get to school.

Johnnie was secretly thinking of throwing a party for Mark's accomplishments and couldn't stop pondering sneaky ways to find a way to get some alcohol to the party.

At lunch time, Johnnie shared with Priscilla, "Hey, let's throw a party for Mark and celebrate his accomplishments."

Priscilla said, "Awesome idea, where are we going to get the booze?"

They both chuckled and began to brainstorm ideas throughout the rest of the day on how to get some alcohol.

Evening time finally rolls in as Johnnie is catching up on homework doing some last-minute studying before going to bed. As he reaches for his soda, he notices his phone begins to vibrate on the table, he sees its Priscilla calling him. He leans over and hits the *"accept call"* button and hears, "Hey Johnnie, my older brother said he'd buy us some alcohol for Mark's party."

"Oh great," Johnnie replied, "The party will be this Friday. Well go to Romero's fine dining restaurant and party in style. I mean after all, we have to learn how to act like adults sooner or later huh?"

Priscilla chuckles and says, "Yeah, it'll be fun."

Johnnie says, "I can make us up some fake ID cards that say were twenty-one so we can order some champagne at Romero's."

"Woo hoo, sounds great!" Priscilla replied. "I have got access to my Aunts house. She is out of town for two weeks. She has a swimming pool and a hot tub. We can go hang out over there after Romero's. I am going to look great for ya Johnnie, be ready for a great night. Gotta go, see ya bye." As usual she quickly hangs up.

Johnnie did not even get a chance to say goodbye, but he sure is smiling.

Early Friday morning Johnnie is leaping off his doorstep to meet with Mark who is going to pick him up for school again. While still shoving a breakfast muffin in his mouth he notices his old childhood friend who is walking down the sidewalk. "Hey Silas, how have you been doing man?"

"Pretty good Johnnie, haven't seen ya in a while."

"Yeah I've been pretty busy with school and stuff, you know."

"Yeah I understand" said Silas. "Hey, I am going to be speaking in Church this Sunday and was wondering if you might want to go?"

"Oh man, you're going to church? Well that is cool, I guess. Anyways, I can't make it Silas, I'm sorry man."

"I understand Johnnie, I'll be praying for you okay."

Johnnie looks kind of shocked thinking to himself, "He's praying for me?" Sensing for the first time in his life that something in his life is missing. Not understanding this sudden empty feeling, he throws up half a smile and replies, "Okay, thanks, i'll see ya later man." As he is thinking to himself, "I probably need to be thinking of church."

Just then Johnnie hears the cool deep roar of the Mustang's motor rolling down the road with the music cranked up. Johnnie's thoughts begin to turn to "Man that car looks good, dark blue paint with the white racing stripes on it."

"Hey, whas up? -Johnnie be good." Mark says laughingly out the window. Then Mark looks at Johnnie again as he seems a bit distraught, "What's wrong man, everything okay?"

Johnnie was thinking about Silas talking about church. Remembering him saying he was going to be praying for him. Then experiencing a strange empty feeling he has never had before. But he kept it silent and replied, "Yeah man everything's great."

Johnnie smiles and jumps in the Mustang and says, "Okay man, we're taking the girls to Romero's tonight for some fine dining. Then were gonna hit Priscilla's aunt's house and her swimming pool since her aunt is out of town. We'll have the house all to ourselves, with the girls!"

"Ha, ha, man, when did ya arrange all this Johnnie?"

"It's all taken care of man, all taken care of. It's going to be a great night." Mark cranks up the music, spins the tires as they cruise to school.

Upon arriving Johnnie quickly finds Priscilla and asks if everything is still on for the night.

With a big grin she says, "Yes, and I can't wait. I went over to my Aunt's last night to make sure the key was still under the plant and checked the pool temperature, the hot tub, and everything is working. Also, the fridge is full of beer and there is some whiskey in the cupboard. And it's only going to be us four."

Johnnie says, "Great, Mark's going to pick me up at five thirty and well come get ya."

"Okay," says Priscilla. "That should give me enough time to pick up my new dress I ordered. I should be ready by five thirty."

"Wow, a new dress huh, for me?" Johnny asks with a big grin like a young child seeing a large wrapped gift under a Christmas tree.

"No, not for you," Priscilla replied, "It's for me silly." She leans up smiling, gives him a quick kiss on the cheek and turns to go to class.

When the school's lunch bell rang, Johnnie, Mark, Priscilla, and Rebecca all met out in the foyer to eat and discuss the evening plans. The close friends vowed not to tell anybody about tonight's celebration. Even though they were some of the most popular kids in school, they trusted each other more than anyone else. The group had grown up together and had always been there for each other. Through the good, and the bad times. They shared a priceless relationship with each other.

After arriving home from school, Johnnie's running through his house in full throttle. With his heart pounding, rushing to get ready for the fun evening that awaits.

His mom says, "Wow, What's the big rush Johnnie? You are acting as if you just hit the lottery or something."

"No, I'm just going to hang out with Mark tonight and if it's okay with you, I was going to crash at his house?"

"Well, I don't see why not. Just make sure you call if you need anything and check in every once in a while to let me know you're alright. You know how I worry."

"Will do mom," says Johnnie.

They hear Mark's pipes screaming out of the back of his Mustang as he pulls into the driveway of Johnnie's house honking the horn. Johnnie's mom meets him out front saying with a big grin, "You better drive careful with my son in that car."

Mark chuckles, "Will do mom."

Johnnie comes flying outside and gives his mom a kiss and says, "Don't worry Mom, we'll be fine, and I'll call to check in."

"You better, you don't want to make me mad. I'll hunt you two down and kick your butts."

As usual, with the music cranked up they speed off to get Priscilla and Rebecca. As they are driving off Johnnie tells Mark that he had arranged to pick up the girls at Rebecca's since her parents were not home.

Johnnie says, "The girls can't tell their parents they are hanging out with us all night. Priscilla told her parents they were going to be at Rebecca's and Rebecca told her parent's they were going to be at Priscilla's."

"Man, that's the dumbest lie," exclaims Mark. "They're bound to get busted. Suppose one parent checks with the other?"

"Well Priscilla said they arranged it, so their parents won't know and not to worry about it, so let's just have fun."

"Alright man, we will certainly do that!" Mark says with a big grin of excitement.

As they pull into Rebecca's driveway honking the horn. Johnnie and Mark both look at each other grinning from ear to ear. They simultaneously pulled some binaca from their tuxedo pockets and sprayed it in their mouth, so they will have fresh breath. They are looking at each other as though they are the luckiest guys in town.

Priscilla and Rebecca were still inside making sure their deodorant wasn't leaving any streaks. Rebecca's in front of the mirror and says to Priscilla, "Dang it, why does my hair always have a mind of its own on a big date night?"

"Would you quit worrying" says Priscilla, "It always looks that bad."

They both laugh and walk out to meet the boys in the Mustang and cruise off to Romero's fine dining restaurant.

In the parking lot of Romero's, Johnnie distributes the ID cards he made up and they all look kind of nervous. Priscilla says, "Are ya all sure this is a good idea? I really don't need my mom picking me up from jail tonight."

Rebecca laughs, "Yeah, that's just what we need."

Johnnie says, "Even if we do get caught, the worst they're going to do is confiscate the fake ID's and kick us out. Now just look confident and let's have some fun. After all, ya only live once."

Priscillas attention goes to noticing the little white lights wrapped around the palm trees, the beautiful landscaping with nicely set water fountains and the candles glistening on the tables through the large windows of the restaurant. She says, "Wow, this place looks really nice."

"Not as good as you." Says Johnnie.

"Woo, smooth one big hitter." Laughs Mark.

As they approach the doors, they soon realize they will have to show they are twenty-one just to get in.

Priscilla begins to get extremely nervous. Mark and Rebecca are whispering, "It's going to be alright, now just calm down."

Johnnie says, "We can go somewhere else if you'd like."

"No, that's okay, let's do it." Says Priscilla as she digs deep to find courage and determination.

Now the decision was final, there was no turning back.

As they are approaching the door. Johnnie is expressing confidence as he walks toward the distinguished looking gentleman at the front counter and says, "Good evening, I have a table for four under Worthington."

"Okay" says the gentleman with a straight face as if he were the FBI himself. "I'll need to see some photo ID from you all."

Poor little Priscilla is now looking as though she is about to cry and have a nervous breakdown. Johnnie pulls out his I.D. first and boldly places it in the man's hand. The man at the door reviews it, makes eye contact with Johnnie, and says, "Enjoy your evening."

Then Priscilla, with her heart pounding and hands shaking gives the straight-faced gentleman her ID. She is feeling certain this is not going to work. The man glances over it and hands it back to her then quickly reaches over to see Mark and Rebecca's I.D. As they also made it in, they are grinning from ear to ear feeling like big shots in Romero's as they are being led to their table by a hostess.

The first thing Johnnie does as they are seated is order a bottle of champagne from their waiter. Johnnie confidently orders a bottle of Nectar Imperial Rose for fifty-six dollars and says with a big grin on his face, "Don't worry ya'll, money is not an object tonight."

Priscilla laughs and jokingly says, "Yeah, it's the cheapest bottle in here." They all begin to chuckle grinning from ear to ear. As they are about to enjoy the night of their lives and celebrate their accomplishments. Feeling prepared and confident to conquer success in the world.

After polishing off three bottles, and a few tasty appetizers Johnnie is ready for the night of romance to begin on the dance floor. With candles glittering on the nice white tablecloths, and the band playing some soft romantic music. Johnnie asks Priscilla if she wants to dance. Wearing her glittery evening gown and her mom's long shiny diamond earrings with matching sparkling necklace she happily says, "I'd love to Johnnie."

While on the dance floor Johnnie starts debating within himself on the decision to express to Priscilla how much he really loves her. He decides he is going to say it. "I'm going to tell her, I'm going to tell her," he thinks to himself. As their eyes meet Johnnie's heart begins to beat rapidly with excitement and nervousness simultaneously as he says, "Priscilla, I really love you and I want to spend the rest of my life with you."

Priscilla is shocked! She thinks this seems a little out of the blue. She had never seen Johnnie serious like this before. However, she secretly and deeply shared the same feelings toward him. She holds back the tears of joy and her emotions the best she can. Feeling a bit shy she says, "That's just the alcohol speaking," While she tries to hide her excitement with a silly smile.

"No," Johnnie says sternly, "I mean it, I really do love you Priscilla, I always have."

Priscilla can no longer hold back as she says, "I love you too Johnnie. I have for a long time." As they intently look into each other's watery eyes experiencing a deep emotion of love for their first time together as they continue dancing slowly.

Meanwhile, back at the table Mark seems to already have a little buzz going on. He cracks a joke about a distinguished looking gentleman at next to them regarding his hair.

His hair resembled the old actor named Fabio. Giggling Rebecca says, "Shh, I think he heard you." Now neither of them can seem to stop laughing.

"Oh no," whispers Rebecca through her laughing. "He's coming over here."

With their faces turning bright red as the man approaches Mark, the man says, "I don't appreciate your jokes about me young man. Please try to handle your alcohol like an adult."

Rebecca is trying not to laugh as she is also feeling embarrassed from the scene that Mark just caused.

Mark says, "Please excuse me sir, we're just out trying to have a good time and we don't want any trouble."

The man is expressing that he is very upset stares at Mark and says, "I am going to go sit back at my table."

"Okay Fabio, have a good night." Replies Mark with a big grin.

With this said, the man was so upset his face turned bright red as he turned to return to his table.

Rebecca kicks Mark under the table and says laughingly, "Behave yourself!"

"Okay Rebecca, C'mon, let's go dance." He stands and takes her by the hand and leads her to the dance floor. They notice that Johnnie and Priscilla are kissing passionately on the dance floor, laughing and flirting kind of loudly. While Johnnie slowly spins Priscilla, he loses grip on her hand and tries to catch her. He stumbles into an older couple. While trying to avoid knocking the older gentleman down Johnnie loses his balance and slips and hits the floor himself!

Mark and Rebecca are now laughing out loud at Johnnie's embarrassing fall. They notice they're being approached by one of the hostess' who says, "We're going to have to ask you all to leave quietly. If you cause a scene, the police will be here in just a couple minutes to escort you all out. Now please leave."

Priscilla is trying to help Johnnie up off the floor, embarrassed and laughing uncontrollably at the same time.

Mark says to the hostess, "Yes sir well leave right now. Sorry for the inconvenience."

As their approaching the door to leave, the hostess asks, "You're not driving I hope."

"Oh no sir" says Mark, "We took a cab and he'll be here shortly after we call him to pick us up."

As their leaving Romero's they notice the hostess is not watching them anymore, so they make their way to the Mustang to drive to Rebecca's aunt's house.

As their flying down the highway Johnnie says, "Man hit the next gas station, I need an energy drink."

As they pull into a Stop and Go corner store with barred windows and graffiti painted on the walls, they realize that they are certainly not in the safest neighborhood in Los Angeles.

Priscilla says, "Maybe we should go somewhere else."

Johnnie says, "Don't worry, it'll only take a second."

As Johnnie gets out of the Mustang to go into the Stop and Go, he notices a group of kids who are dressed like gang members checking out the Mustang and the girls who are all dressed up.

Rebecca notices even Mark is looking a little nervous. "Man, what is taking Johnnie so long?" Whispers Mark.

"I don't know but I wish he'd hurry up," says Rebecca.

The gang members are staring at the car. The lead gang member starts walking in their direction. He approaches the car with his three friends and says, "Hey whaz up essay, y'all in the wrong neighborhood homes."

With Priscilla and Rebecca looking scared to death, Rebecca quickly reaches up and locks the doors.

Johnnie is now at the counter purchasing some red bulls and a bottle of Jack Daniels. He notices that the Mustang has four gang members standing at the drivers' side door harassing Mark. He exits the store and speedily heads toward the car.

Rebecca jumps in the back seat and opens the door so Johnnie can get in quickly. One of the gang members starts hitting the window and kicking the door as he's yelling, "whaz up man, stupid rich kids coming into my hood!"

Johnnie dives in the passenger side and Mark slams it in first gear and floors it, almost hitting one of the gang members.

"Dang it man!" yells Mark, "I probably got a dent in my door. What took you so long Johnnie?"

"Man, I'm sorry Mark, I had no idea." Johnnie replies.

After a deep breath of relief as they are safely approaching the highway, Mark says with a makeshift grin, "It's cool man, nothing like a little excitement on our big night out on the town."

Mark and Johnnie look at each other and grin. With this grin they both know that everything is cool between them.

"Alright man,,, let's partyyyy!" yells Mark.

The girls in the back seat, are still shaken up a little, they slowly begin to relax. Thankful that everything worked out as well as it did considering the circumstances. Priscilla looks at Rebecca and says, "Told ya we would have a fun night."

The boys are laughing, then the girls started laughing and all is good on the way to Rebecca's aunt's house.

"Give me one of those red bulls Johnnie," says Mark.

Johnnie pulls out the drinks and passes them out so they each had one.

"Oh, I love this song," says Rebecca. "Turn it up."

As they're flying down the road with the cool California night air coming in the windows and sunroof. With all their troubles now seemingly gone. Suddenly they notice flashing red and blue lights reflecting from their back side.

"Darn it!" Says Mark, "just what I needed. I'm going to get a DUI and my cars going to get towed."

The good feeling of the music and the California night air blowing through the windows is instantly gone. Mark pulls over and says, "Just act cool guys."

The police car pulls over behind them, and after two minutes of what seemed like a half-hour the police officer exits his squad car and begins to approach the Mustang. Mark and Johnnie are looking nervous as were the girls.

Johnnie quietly sighs and says, "Okay God if you're real, please get us out of this mess."

Mark watches the officer approach through his side mirror. The police officer stops and gets on his radio. Then he yells to Mark, "This is your lucky day. I just got a domestic call. Slow down and drive careful."

"Yes sir, thank you officer," Mark says out the window.

As they drive off, Priscilla says, "Wow Johnnie, looks like God answered your prayer."

Johnnie has a serious look on his face as if he believes God really did answer his prayer.

26

Johnnie has a quick flashback of his conversation with Silas who said to him, "I'll be praying for you Johnnie."

28

Chapter Two
Johnnies Departure

They finally arrive at Rebecca's aunt's house. As they're pulling into the driveway Mark turns off the Mustang and says, "Wow, we made it this far without getting busted at the restaurant, not getting robbed by the gang, and avoiding a DUI, thanks to Johnnie's prayer." As he reaches over and messes up Johnnie's hair with a laugh.

"Man Mark," says Johnnie, "I'm glad that worked out the way it did. We don't need any trouble coming in the way of our careers in the future."

Mark replies, "Yeah, I heard ya there, anyways, we're here now and I'm sure insurance can fix that small dent in my door."

As Johnnie and Priscilla enter the kitchen area Johnnie opens the Jack Daniels and quickly puts down three shots.

Priscilla says, "Hey Johnnie why don't ya slow it down a bit, are you crazy." As she fakes a grin, not wanting to offend him.

Mark and Rebecca are already in the hot tub enjoying the weather and another glass of champagne.

Priscilla says to Johnnie, "Hey, let's go get in our swimsuits and relax in the hot tub, c'mon, it'll be fun."

"Okay" says Johnnie.

As Priscilla heads upstairs Johnnie is still thinking this party is going to be all the better if he has more to drink. So he hurries and sneaks in three more quick shots of Jack Daniels. "Man, this stuff isn't too hard to gut down," he thinks to himself. He stumbles into the bathroom to get on his swim trunks and returns to the hot tub area outside where Priscilla had already arrived. Johnnie jumps in and takes a seat. Feeling the warm water, the alcohol seems to instantly take effect. He notices everything seemed to be spinning out of control. Feeling sick to his stomach all the sudden, as though he is going to throw up.

Johnnie is battling thoughts of feeling embarrassed for ruining this night because he had too much to drink. He is also getting nervous about the way he is feeling physically.

"Hey Mark, Priscilla, I'm not feeling real good man," Johnnie murmurs. "I think I'm going to go lay down."

"Oh, c'mon Johnnie, I know that old trick. C'mon, stay and hang out for a while," says Mark.

"Yeah Johnnie, please stay," says Priscilla, "this is nice."

Johnnie says, "I can't," as he hurries and stumbles out of the hot tub. Johnnie makes it into the dining room and collapses on the floor.

"I'm sorry Priscilla," says Rebecca, "I'm sure he'll get feeling better so y'all can enjoy the night. He'll probably be back out in a few minutes."

"Yeah, I'm sure he will" says Priscilla.

With all the fun conversations about the excitement of the night they had lost track of time. About forty-five minutes later Priscilla says, "Hey, where is Johnnie?"

"Mark, go check on him," says Rebecca, "We will stay here, and bring me a cup of coffee, please."

"Yes ma'am," says Mark with a big grin.

Johnnie is laying on the floor thinking to himself, "Oh my gosh, I feel horrible. I wish this room would quit spinning." Johnnie is starting to feel like he may need an ambulance ride to the hospital. He finally stopped throwing up but is feeling as if breathing is a chore. "Okay, okay, I'll just stare at one spot in the room and try to focus on it. And maybe the room will stop spinning. "Man, why is my heart racing so fast?" Johnnie thinks to himself.

Suddenly out of nowhere he sees two ghostly images dressed in gray that look kind of foggy to him. One is wearing a sash around his chest that says, "*Depression*," and the other one's sash says, "*Misery*."

They are both saying with soft tones, "Johnnie, come with us Johnnie."

"Who are you?" Johnnie asks fearfully.

"We're here to take you home Johnnie," they say.

Johnnie's heart continues to pound as a deep, dark fear grips him like he never could have imagined. "Okay man, keep yourself together" Johnnie thinks to himself, "This alcohol is really messing with me." He quickly notices that somehow, he is instantly sitting at the kitchen table. He looks down and sees what could be his twin lying on the floor surrounded with vomit. The kid on the floor is also wearing a sash that says, "*un-believer*." "What the heck is going on?" He mutters to himself.

Johnnie sees Mark coming in laughing, "Wow Johnnie, who's going to clean this mess?" Mark softly and jokingly kicks the guy on the floor. Johnnie yells, "Mark, I'm right here man!"

Mark ignores him as if he can't hear him and kneels on the floor next to the kid who looks just like Johnnie.

Rebecca and Priscilla come running in and kneel next to him on the floor as well. Johnnie starts getting these crazy thoughts, "Is that me on the floor?"

"Oh my gosh, oh my gosh, No, it can't be." As his heart is thumping, he starts yelling, "Priscilla I'm right here! Why are you ignoring me?" Johnnies vision zooms in closer on the kid his three friends have surrounded and clearly sees, this is no joke! "That is me," as his thoughts are arrested, his whole being is full of fear and darkness. He can see Priscilla is doing CPR and Mark is calling 911. Johnnie watches as *"depression"* and *"misery"* are coming up out of the floor repeatedly saying with a smooth eeeri tone, "Johnnie, we're here to get you now, Johnnie we're here to get you now." Johnnie's heart is pounding as if it were going to come out of his chest. The amount of fear and darkness he is experiencing seems to permeate his very soul. Also, as *depression* and *misery* approach closer to Johnnie, he notices they are seemingly floating. As he can see them more clearly, he notices one thing. That they hate him and are excited to bring extreme torment to him. They get close enough to grab Johnnie and begin to bite and scratch at him. They have the ugliest, scariest most evil look on their face. Johnnie even notices they have a horrible odor proceeding from their being.

In the middle of Johnnie's unimaginable fear and torment he is instantly back in his body. Looking up, he notices he is in an ambulance with some paramedics leaning over him. Johnnie hears the paramedics say, "We got a heartbeat back."

He looks over and sees Priscilla sitting there holding his hand saying, "Johnnie, calm down, what are you screaming and kicking for?"

Johnnie was glad to realize they were there working on him. Really glad to see Priscilla at his side. He now believes everything is going to be okay. He begins to relax again. Johnnie slowly closes his eyes as his sleepiness seems to be getting the best of him.

As Johnnie closes his eyes again, he is instantly back in that dark room with *misery* and *depression* who hate him.

They begin demanding, "Johnnie, its time to come with us Johnnie."

Johnnie yells, "Who are you? How do you know my name? Leave me alone!" Johnnie's heart continues to race uncontrollably as if it were going to explode again. "Why don't you leave me alone?" Johnnie cries loudly, "leave me alone!"

Instantly he hears a loud scream, saying, "Johnnie," but this time it is Priscilla's voice. Once again Johnnie is in an ambulance and again hears the paramedic saying, "We got the heartbeat back."

Again, Johnnie looks over and sees Priscilla crying at his side. Johnnie is freaking out wondering if he is going to die or not. Johnnie begins to cry, thinking to himself how much he wants to live. He realizes how precious life is.

Johnnie hears one of the paramedics say, "okay we're here. Dr Graham has been notified that Johnnie is coming in and should have everything ready."

The paramedic says to Priscilla, "Honey, you're going to have to wait out here for a little while."

As Johnnie is being wheeled out of the ambulance and into the hospital. His mom arrives and came up with tears streaming down her cheeks. Leaning over him and says, "I love you Johnnie, I love you."

37

As Johnnie is being wheeled through the hall at a relatively good rate of speed by a paramedic who must have been a track star. Johnnie notices it seems as though suddenly the hospital lights went out and it went completely dark. He now has this sensation that he is falling, full force, down a dark tunnel surrounded with a wall of rocks. Johnnie notices a horrible smell of sulfur whirling through this tunnel as he falls. With his heart feeling as though it is coming out of his chest. Johnnie is now falling rapidly into darkness. Full of fear he has never even been able to imagine, wondering, "Why am I falling so quickly?" Johnnie lets out a horrendous scream as he notices a huge ball of fire, explosions and thick smoke as he is falling rapidly into some sort of lake of fire or hot lava. With his heart pounding and his mind racing, Johnnie has never even been able to imagine such terror.

He notices below that there are people in these flames. As he gets closer to the flames, he can hear them screaming with pure terror in their voices. He then notices what must be a fifteen-foot-tall dragon type creature with large powerful wings screaming like an eagle coming right at him! With scales strong like armor, and razor-sharp teeth, wearing a sash that says, "*hatred*." This creature attaches himself to Johnnie with eagle like claws. "What the, what the, what is going on?" Johnnie screams in excruciating pain, agony, and deep fear.

Instantly he hears Priscilla's voice screaming his name. That at this point, is the most beautiful sound in the world. Johnnie is back in the hospital and sees Priscilla is looking at him as if she can't believe what is going on.

Johnnie musters the strength to say, "What is going on?"

Priscilla says, "Johnnie you are kicking and screaming on that bed and the Dr's can't seem to keep your heartbeat going. You've got to calm down. Why are you acting so scared?"

Johnnie is crying and has the most horrified look on his face. He doesn't know how to explain to Priscilla what he just experienced. He is absolutely horrified.

Dr Graham walks in and says, "Okay everyone is going to have to wait outside so we can work on Johnnie."

This is not what Johnnie wants to hear but cannot even find the strength to say anything else. He notices everyone leaving as Dr Graham administers some more medicine into his I.V tube. As Johnnie seems to relax a bit, he hears a loud thud and it sounds as if something is scratching violently at the door.

Johnnie opens his eyes and there is *"hatred."* The fifteen-foot-tall dragon, with his eagle like claws flying directly at him. Johnnie can feel the force of the wind coming from hatred's wings as hatred is screaming like a loud violent eagle would scream.

Johnnie screams in complete agony and fear, as his heart again begins to pound as if it were going to come out of his chest. This beast has locked Johnnie in its grips and is descending toward this dark pit again and reaches even closer to the flames than last time. Johnnie is hoping to hear Priscilla's voice like before but cannot seem to hear anything except all the people screaming in that fire of agony.

He heard one girl in the flames yelling, "Don't come here, there is no way out."

Johnnie is released by this powerful beast as he slams into this lake of fire. He lets out the most blood curling cry, as this pain is unimaginable. Johnnie thinks to himself, "It feels as if acid and fire are burning right through me. Why am I not dying? What is going on?" As he cannot stop screaming. Johnnie realizes that there is no time here. All hope is gone, all peace is gone, and this agonizing pain of this burning fire will not stop.

Back at the hospital the alarm in room 316 begins beeping as it cannot detect a heartbeat. Dr Graham calls for more assistants to help in the room. Johnnie's mom and friends are starting to wonder if Johnnie is going to die.

"Oh my gosh," cries Priscilla, "I loved him so much, I was hoping we would get married."

"Don't talk like that" snaps Janice, "you're talking as if he is already dead."

"I'm sorry Janice." Replies Priscilla.

Mark is just sitting in unbelief. Thinking he could have done something to stop Johnnie from drinking so much.

Mark notices the kid Johnnie was talking to on the sidewalk the other day when he picked him up for school. "Except, why is he wearing a nursing gown?" Mark thinks to himself.

This kid walks up to Mark and says, "Hey I remember you, you're the kid with the really cool Mustang who picked up Johnnie for school the other day, hi my name is Silas. Why are you here man, is everything okay?" asks Silas.

"No man," replies Mark, "Johnnie and I were partying tonight, and Johnnie had too much to drink and may die of alcohol poisoning. His heart just stopped again for like the third or fourth time and they just went running in his room to try to revive him."

"What room is he in?" Silas asked, expressing authority on his face.

"He is in room 316 Silas, whatever you can do to help him man, please do."

Silas replies with a serious look on his face, "You must pray!"

Silas quickly grabs his cell phone and dials. Mark overhears the conversation.

Silas says, "Hello Pastor Timothy, I need you down here with me at the Emergency Room immediately. Johnnie that kid we have been praying for is fighting for his life right now.

Please hurry and have someone call the prayer chain. Thank you Pastor, drive safe." Silas does not even say bye, he just closes his phone and runs to Johnnie's room.

Mark slowly follows Silas since he seems to be acting as if he has some kind of antidote to help his dying friend Johnnie.

Mark sees that Silas is terribly upset with the staff for not letting him in Johnnie's room to pray. He is almost causing a scene. Mark approaches Silas, "Hey man, just calm down. Let the doctors do their thing okay, I'm worried about him too."

Silas just looks at him with that same authoritative look that left Mark feeling kind of insignificant just a few moments ago.

Silas just begins to pray loudly and passionately, *"Oh God, in the name of Jesus Christ, I come to you and ask you to have mercy on my friend Johnnie. I've been praying for him for some time God, please don't let him go God."*

44

Mark notices some men with Bibles coming toward them. One of them says, "C'mon Silas let's go in this waiting room and pray."

"Okay Pastor Timothy," replies Silas, "Hey Mark, why don't you come with us and pray for Johnnie okay."

Mark says, "Well, I don't think so man. I better go be with his family and other friends." Mark turns to go back to where Johnnie's mom and the girls were. He sees the Emergency room staff pull a sheet over Johnnie's lifeless body as he passes room 316. "I can't tell them, I can't tell them," Mark thinks to himself. He turns around and enters the room where Silas and the others are praying and just sits in the corner crying. Mark starts to notice that he feels a strange sense of peace listening to these men pray. "Man, they're praying as if they were an army attacking a different nation or something," Mark thinks to himself. "This is kind of weird, why do I seem to feel this strange sense of peace in all that is going on around me?"

Then Dr Graham slowly opens the door and says softly, "I'm really sorry guys, I am truly sorry, we did all we could do."

Silas runs in the room where Johnnie is. The other men who were praying quickly followed. Mark sat up and followed them into room 316 where he saw Johnnie's lifeless form under a sheet.

Silas prays earnestly, *"Lord you came to seek and to save the lost.* [1] *Lord, you also said that you are not willing that any should perish.* [2] *And God I thank you that You so loved the world that You gave Your Son for us* [3] *and that if two or more agree in prayer it will be done for us.* [4] *And that the prayer of faith will save the sick and the Lord will raise him up, and if*

---

[1] Luke 19:10
[2] 2 Peter 3:9
[3] John 3:16
[4] Matthew 18:19

he has committed sins he will be forgiven[5]" Silas grabs the sheet off of Johnnie and starts shaking him demanding, "Get up Johnnie, get up!"

"Hey man, leave him alone" says Mark.

Pastor Timothy puts his hand on Silas's back and says very softly, "C'mon Silas, let's go."

Silas refuses, "No! We are not leaving here without Johnnie! Now pray with faith or back off!"

Meanwhile Johnnie is noticing the thick, horrible smell of sulfur that won't go away. He wishes he had just one drop of water to cool the burning on his tongue.[6] Johnnie begins to realize he is never getting out of this place of torment as he sinks into a deep level of hopelessness. He knows he will never see his loved ones again. And with the intense pain he and all those around him are experiencing he

---

[5] James 5:15
[6] Luke 16:24

knows that he will never again have a moment of peace and quiet.

Chapter Three
A Light in the Darkness

Suddenly Johnnie notices a brilliant powerful light of the purest white he has ever seen descending from the expanse. His eyes are drawn to this light as he notices an image which is in the form of a man inside this great light. The light is getting brighter and brighter as it descends toward Johnnie.

The man in the light approaches closely to Johnnie and reaches out His hand and says, "Come with Me, it's not yet your time Johnnie." He expresses with much authority and tenderness. Johnnie notices His eyes are full of strength, love and authority. As Johnnie grabs His hand, all the pain is instantly gone.

The hopelessness is instantly gone. Johnnie is overcome with tears of joy and asks, "Who are you?"

"I am Jesus." He says, "It's not yet your time, you must return Johnnie."

Johnnie notices His pant legs are labeled,

"*King of kings, Lord of lords*"

As Johnnie is hoping he can always stay in Jesus' grasp he instantly is being shaken by his friend in room 316 in the hospital. Johnnie takes a deep breath as his eyes open! Silas about has a heart attack, realizing God answered his prayer.

"He's alive!" Silas yells at the top of his lungs, "He's alive," with his words "He's alive" echoing down the hallway of the hospital, a nurse close by calls for Dr Graham who comes in and starts to examine Johnnie.

Johnnie's mom and Priscilla are outside the room with tears of joy streaming down their face as they begin to hope again.

Mark runs out and hugs them and says, "He is going to make it!"

Johnnie was dead for 25 minutes. Johnnie's heart rate and vital signs slowly begin to recover and balance out. The I.V is placed back in just to keep him hydrated.

Doctor Graham asks Johnnie, "Is there anything I can do for you?"

Johnnie cries, "Yes doctor, please let me see Priscilla, let me see Priscilla."

Priscilla, just outside the door hears those words and runs in to be at Johnnie's side and leans over him crying with tears of joy. She says, "You're going to make it Johnnie, you're going to make it. I was so scared".

Johnnie doesn't say anything but just stares at Priscilla. He is glad to have her laying her head on his chest and being able to hear her voice. Johnnie falls into a deep sleep and doesn't wake up for 13 hours. As he sleeps the doctor's team continually notice that Johnnie is recovering very speedily. They tell his mom Janice that Johnnie will have a complete miraculous recovery and will more than likely be home in one or two days. "We just want to keep him here a little while longer to make sure everything stays in balance." The doctor tells Janice.

The next day the hospital releases Johnnie who gets to go home with his mom. Still tired from the excitement he starts realizing how much he had put his mom through.

"I'm really sorry mom, I didn't think this would happen." Johnnie says with his head hung low expressing shame.

"Johnnie that was the worst night of my life, I love you so much I'm just glad you're okay." Says his mom.

"Me too," Johnnie says. As Johnnie walks into his house his depression now seems unbearable. He was not sure about all he had experienced the night before. One thing he was sure of is that it was not just dreams, but that what he had experienced was real. These thoughts terrified Johnnie and he knew that he would never be the same again. Everything he had enjoyed so much before seemed so insignificant to him now.

Johnnie tried to watch the UCLA ball game on television, but his mind kept returning to what happened last night. He wanted to call Priscilla but knew he wasn't the same ole happy go lucky Johnnie. He did not want her to know he was depressed, and he had no idea how he was ever going to be able to explain to his friends what happened to him.

Two long weeks have passed. Mark, Rebecca, and Priscilla are starting to worry about Johnnie because he has secluded himself at home and is no longer attending classes or taking their phone calls.

Saturday morning the doorbell rings and Johnnie's mom opens the door.

"Hi Mrs. Kindleton, is Johnnie around? We haven't seen him for a while and would like to see how he's doing."

Janice quickly steps outside and quietly says, "I'm glad you all came by, you're all such good friends. But look, Johnnie has seemed really depressed, maybe embarrassed about what has happened. I'm not sure what he's going through. Maybe you all can cheer him up." She says with a lump in her throat holding back tears as she is obviously saddened by what her son is going through.

Priscilla says, "Johnnie is a strong young man Mrs, Kindleton, he's going to be fine. He probably needs a little time."

"Perhaps you are right Priscilla," Janice replies expressing doubt as she continues, "But he has never secluded himself like this before and all he does is lay in his bedroom. Sometimes he walks around the block a few times. But he doesn't want much conversation."

"Let me go talk to him," says Priscilla as she slides by Janice entering in the front door in route towards Johnnie's room.

Johnnie has no idea his friends are downstairs and wasn't looking forward to any company. He has not showered for a couple of days and has been lying around in his pajamas.

Johnnie hears a knock on his bedroom door.

"Johnnie, its Priscilla, open the door!" She demands.

Johnnie jumps up, feeling a little embarrassed. He grudgingly opens the door and goes and sits back down on his bed. Priscilla quickly notices that Johnnie is not too happy about her being there. Wanting to make sure he is okay, she slowly makes her way over to the bed and sits next to Johnnie. She begins to rub her fingers through the back of his hair and softly says, "Johnnie, I'm worried about you and I want you to know that I'm here for you."

Johnnie is desperate, wanting to tell Priscilla everything he went through that night in the hospital. He refrains because he is convinced that she will think he is losing his mind. He musters up a fake smile and says, "Thank you Priscilla I'm going to be okay."

Mark and Rebecca walk in the room, "Hey whaz-up? Johnnie be good," Mark says trying to cheer up Johnnie.

Johnnie grins and says, "Thanks for coming over, I'll need a little time to shower. Why don't you come pick me up in an hour okay" as he grudgingly agrees to go get some ice cream with them a little later.

"Sounds great man," says Mark.

Priscilla's eyes light up with excitement as she finally gets to spend some time with the boy that she loves.

Johnnie reluctantly gets all cleaned up as he really doesn't feel like going with his friends. He is still scared to death over all that had happened in the hospital.

Johnnie hears the doorbell and goes down to open the door and sees that it is Silas. "Hi Silas" says Johnnie, "how are you doing?"

"I'm ok Johnnie, I just came by to see how you were doing. It looks like you are doing rather good. I just wanted to let you know Johnnie that I am glad everything worked out good for you that night at the hospital. I am here for you if you need anything. I mean anything let me know and don't be shy okay" he says with a big grin and a twinkle in his eye.

"How did you know I went to the hospital?"

"I was there," replied Silas, "I have been doing some nursing classes and have to get hours in, ha, you know, work for free type stuff," he says with a grin. "You don't remember me in your room Johnnie?"

"No, I don't, did I talk to you or see you that night?"

"We'll you were in and out, so I'm not surprised you don't remember. I am just glad you're doing so well. Glad I had the opportunity to be praying for you Johnnie."

Johnnie is thinking of so many questions he wants to ask Silas. As he talks to him, he finally feels a little life come back into him. As Johnnie finally finds the courage to ask Silas if he could go to church with him, he is interrupted when his friends arrive to see if he is ready for ice cream.

Johnnie now regretting he committed to going with them says, "Yeah I'm ready, hey Silas do you want to go?"

"Well do you want me to sit in the trunk?" As he laughs, "No man I don't think there's room and I'm going to meet with the youth group in an hour and a half. Thanks for the offer though."

Silas smiles at his friends as he says, "I got to go, you guys have fun," as he turns to leave.

"Okay Silas, we'll talk to you later," Johnnie says as if he doesn't want him to leave because he wanted to ask more about church.

They all jump in the Mustang and head out to the local fifties diner to get some ice cream and a soda.

Johnnie asks his friends, "Hey did you all see Silas at the hospital that night?"

"Yeah" says Mark, "he was there, he also had his Pastor come and they were all praying for you. Actually, Silas got to the point where he was shaking you and all this crazy stuff, crazy religious people," Mark says laughingly.

Rebecca also starts to laugh, but Priscilla who was sitting in the back seat with Johnnie notices that Johnnie doesn't find it funny at all. They all become silent and uncomfortable for the rest of the ride to the diner.

Arriving at the diner Mark tries to cheer Johnnie up by talking about the Bruins game because he felt kind of bad about his religious joke.

"Yeah I saw part of the game," says Johnnie, "but I missed the last half, who won?"

"Oh, c'mon man you didn't even see the end, since when did you miss a UCLA game?" The bruins won 34 to 20, it was awesome man. By half time it looked like we were going to get our butts kicked but they came back in the third quarter and totally took control of the ball game."

"Sounds great," Says Johnnie as he tries to sound excited.

After another half hour of trying to make things as they used to be and about finished with their ice cream Mark says, "Hey why don't we head out to the beach and throw a Frisbee or do some surfing? I heard the surf is supposed to be great this afternoon."

Johnnie smiles as he says, "Man you guys are awesome, the best friends I've ever had. I'm really sorry but I think I'm going to head home and rest a little more, I still feel really tired."

"No way Johnnie, we're forcing you to go and that's just the way it is," Mark says with a grin. "We've missed ya man and want to spend some time with you."

Johnnie smiles realizing his friends are just trying to cheer him up, he knows he is lacking the ability to be his same old self again.

Priscilla says, "Hey you guys, Johnnie has been through a lot. Let's just take him home so he can rest," with both her little hands holding tightly onto Johnnies hand.

They arrive at Johnnie's house and he says, "Hey you guys thanks again, and I mean it when I say you guys are the best friends I've had."

"Okay man, you're going to have to stop all this sentimental stuff already," Mark says jokingly.

"Don't worry, I'll keep it at that. I just wanted to let you all know that," Johnnie says with a grin.

"C'mon" says Priscilla, "I'll walk you to your door."

As they arrive at Johnnies front door Priscilla asks, "Can I stay and hang out with ya Johnnie? I won't talk too much. I'll just hang out on your couch and try not to make too much slurping noise with my soda, C'mon, Johnnie I promise I won't even make fun of you for spilling that ice cream on your shirt."

"Ha," Johnnie laughs, "Sure come on in."

"Great!" Says Priscilla as she waves off Mark and Rebecca, they enter Johnnie's living room.

Janice walks in, "Oh hello Priscilla welcome back you two. How did it go?"

"Oh it went great Mrs. Kindle ton, except Johnnie spilt some ice cream on his shirt."

"Hey," says Johnnie, "you promised."

"Yeah we'll, I lied, I couldn't resist I promise it won't happen again, today anyways." Priscilla says laughingly.

"Well alright, I am going upstairs to finish painting the bedroom," says Janice, "You all holler if you need anything."

"Okay mom, will do," says Johnnie as he sits on the couch and picks up the television remote and begins to channel surf. He stops on a channel that is talking about the Bible.

The first thing he hears the preacher saying is, *"God Almighty has a plan for your life!"*

Johnnie is stunned. These words seem as if they are alive to him, as if the man on the television said that just for him. Johnnie seems to lose interest in everything around him as he turns up the volume a little bit.

The preacher on the screen was staring into the camera and said, *"You're lost in your sin, you're separated from a loving God and you're searching for anything to fill that void in your life and you can't find it! You've tried alcohol, you've tried all different kinds of things, but you know something is missing in your life. Everyone else around you is living as if everything is fine and dandy, but you know something is missing. I'm here to tell you that Jesus Christ died on a cross for your sin.[7] He (Jesus) who knew no sin became sin for us that we may be made the righteousness of God in Him.[8] Jesus Christ is the Lamb who was slain for us.[9] I'm telling you that He loves you. The Bible says, Greater love has no one than this than to lay down his life for his friends.[10] And that is exactly what Jesus Christ did for you."*

Johnnie is almost on the edge of the couch hanging on to every word this preacher is saying

---

[7] John 3:16
[8] 2 Corinthians 5:21
[9] John 1:36
[10] John 15:13

as if he can't get enough. "Man," Johnnie thinks, "Has he been reading my mail?"

Priscilla is observing him from the kitchen wondering about this new side of Johnnie she has never seen before. Priscilla slowly walks over and sits next to Johnnie and doesn't say a word. Johnnie inwardly is a little embarrassed, but his curiosity is strong enough to not worry too much about what Priscilla thinks of him watching a preacher.

After the program Johnnie turns off the television and looks at Priscilla and says, "What do you think of all that?"

"I don't know anything about religion Johnnie, except it seems like the few religious people I have met seem pretty happy. On the other hand, it also seems like it can be a boring lifestyle. What do you think about all of it? I mean aren't there so many different religions? What do you do, just find one that best meets your needs and join that one? What is religion really for anyways? I mean, as long as you're a pretty good person I don't think you need a religion to be good. Were fairly good kids, were not perfect but compared to a lot of people were doing alright. We've only really partied that one time and I don't think any of us want to do that again."

"Yeah that isn't no joke," says Johnnie with a shallow grin.

"You know Johnnie on the serious side I remember that night on the dance floor, well, do you remember what you said?"

"Oh absolutely Priscilla. The alcohol may have given me the courage to say it, but it was really me talking. As I was laying there wondering if I was ever going to see you again in the hospital it was tearing me apart Priscilla."

"Johnnie, I love you too." Says Priscilla, "I just want you to know that, and if you want to join a religion that is fine with me. I just want to be here for you."

Johnnie's heart melts as he softly says, "Wow Priscilla, I think you're my angel." There is so much I want to share with you about that night."

As Johnnie finally feels its time to share with Priscilla what happened he is interrupted with his mom saying, "Are you kid's hungry?"

Johnnie and Priscilla both wiping their teary eyes because of the serious conversation they were in, gather themselves together and simultaneously say, "Yeah, what's for dinner?"

They can't help but smile at each other. Johnnies mom says, "The pizza man just showed up. He should be knocking at the door any second now."

As Johnnie goes to get the pizza Priscilla's phone rings. After getting the pizza Johnnie comes back into the living room.

Priscilla says, "I'm sorry, I've got to go. That was my mom, she needs me to babysit. I'm starving, can I steal a piece of pizza for the road?"

"Certainly can, do you need a ride?"

"No thanks, my mom is already out front. Well see ya later okay Johnnie."

"Okay Priscilla, have a good night, bye."

"Well you two seem to be getting kind of serious," says his mom.

"Yeah, looks like it doesn't it." Replies Johnnie.

"She really seems to like you Johnnie, and I think she's a real nice girl."

"Yeah so do I mom," says Johnnie. "Hey mom, off the subject, what do you know about religion?"

"Preachers want your money Johnnie. All roads lead to heaven if you're a good person. Are you asking because of what you went through?"

"Well honestly yes, that is more than likely what got me thinking about it."

Johnnie's mom says, "Most religious people seem so judgmental about others don't they?"

"We'll not really, Silas is pretty religious and he's actually a pretty cool guy."

"That's true," says Johnnies mom.

After eating a piece of pizza Johnnie begins to head upstairs to his room.

"Are you just going to have one piece of pizza Johnnie? That doesn't seem like you, not much of an appetite tonight huh?"

"No not really mom, I think I'm going to go to bed early."

As Johnnie heads upstairs he doesn't know what he is going to do with the amount of depression he is experiencing. Although Priscilla helped get his mind off everything he's been through. He feared it would never be enough.

knowing he faked many smiles throughout his time with her. Though loving her he knew he needed something more and could not stop thinking about the level of terror he experienced that night he died at the hospital. As Johnnie goes to lie down to try to sleep, he begins to wrestle with his thoughts and cannot seem to stop worrying about life after death.

"Man, is that where I'm heading when I die? Why were there so many people suffering there? There must have been millions in that volcano like lake of fire." Johnnie begins tossing and turning as he is wrestling in his bed. He thinks to himself, "Man, it's almost as if "*depression and misery*" are right here with me." Out of the corner of his eye Johnnie sees what appears to be depression or misery walk through the corner of his room. Johnnie thinks to himself,

"Is my mind playing tricks on me?"

Johnnie saw this ghostly image was wearing a sash with a nametag on it. He was unable to make out what it said. Johnnie is wishing he could take some sort of sleeping pill to stop his mind from racing. And through his turmoil Johnnie cries out loud,

"God please help me!" Instantly he feels relieved from his fear. He feels peace as if it had literally filled his room. Johnnie is astonished and lays his head back down on his pillow and finally falls asleep. Johnnie wakes up twelve hours later and can hardly believe how long he slept without a nightmare. Then he remembers the peace that saturated his room right after crying out to God. "Wow, it feels so good to have a solid night's sleep without a nightmare," Johnnie thinks to himself. He has not had a night without a nightmare since the night at the hospital.

Chapter four
Freedom from the chains

After experiencing a good night's sleep Johnnie finally has a little hope that his days of depression may be over. "I think I'll just go for a walk today and get ready to return to school tomorrow," Johnnie thinks to himself. After getting cleaned up he leashes up Scout and heads for the park with Scout's favorite toss toy.

Arriving at the park Johnnie begins once again experiencing this cloud of depression hanging over him. Johnnie thinks to himself, "This is so horrible I can barely handle it," As he loses interest in playing with Scout. He decides to stick it out anyway and try to make the best of the day.

Johnnie throws Scout's toss toy as far as he can and has Scout sit and stay until he gives the command, "fetch it up boy." Scout takes off heading for the toy and ends up running through the thick brush in the park. Johnnie figures he better go looking for his dog. Now not only feeling depressed, but also getting a bit angry as he walks through the woods yelling his dog's name. Johnnie feels a dark fearful feeling that seems to be surrounding him. He begins to experience flashbacks of "*hatred*" that dragon like creature that grasped him that night at the hospital. It's as if that thing is there with him but Johnnie can't see it. As Johnnie hears some noise back in the woods, he gets so freaked out that he has goose bumps all over him. Being tormented with thoughts, Johnnie runs out of the woods back into the populated area of the park.

"Man, am I going crazy?" Johnnie asks himself, "Why am I so afraid to look through the woods to find my dog?"

He looks up and sees Scout running toward him with the toss toy in his mouth. Johnnie leashes him up and says, "Come on boy, were going home." Johnnie now feeling more depressed than ever. He realizes that he doesn't have much of a future with this kind of fear and depression. He decides to just separate himself from all his friends and to stop seeing Priscilla because he now believes she will have a better life with someone else. With his depression so heavy, having a lump in in throat, he could not hold back the tears as he walked home from the park, keeping his head down hoping no one he knew would drive by and see him.

As he approaches near home, he notices Silas walking in his direction. Johnnie, feeling embarrassed not wanting to see anybody like this. Now has no way to avoid a conversation with Silas.

"Hey what's up Johnnie?" asks Silas, "Taking Scout out for a walk huh? Nice day for it."

"Yeah we just went over to the park and ran around a bit."

Silas notices that Johnnie has been crying but acts as though he does not because he doesn't want to embarrass Johnnie. Silas says, "Well I'm heading to church if you want to come? I am just offering Johnnie, no need to feel any pressure. I just want you to know you're more than welcome okay."

"Man Silas, I don't know anything about religion. I am not sure what to do there. I was watching a preacher on television the other day and it was almost like he was talking directly to me."

"Ha," Silas laughs, "That happens to me quite a bit Johnnie, ya know it's really not about a religion. It is more about Jesus Christ. He is my source of peace Johnnie. And He is real."

Something clicked in Johnnie when he heard Silas say, *"My source of peace!"*

"Yeah man, I think I want to go with you, are you sure it's okay?"

"Man Johnnie, I'm excited about it, C'mon, I'll go with you to take Scout home."

As Johnnie and Silas walk in the church Johnnie is feeling a little out of place. But at the same time experiencing a sense of excitement and peace like Silas mentioned. About fifteen people approached Johnnie and introduced themselves to him as they made their way into the sanctuary.

Johnnie says to Silas, "Man, you have a lot of friends."

Silas grins, "Yeah this is my home Johnnie, my family."

The Pastor comes up to Johnnie, and shakes his hand and says, "Man it's good to see you here Johnnie. I have not seen you since the night at the hospital. God has a plan for your life Johnnie. It's nice to finally meet you."

"Thank you sir," says Johnnie, as he seemed it kind of weird that the preacher on television said the exact same thing, "God has a plan for your life."

About four people take the stage and each pick up an instrument and start to sing songs like Johnnie has never heard. It sounded wonderful to Johnnie. He just stands there in awe of what he is experiencing. People are lifting their hands and singing along actively as if they were singing to God Himself. "I have never felt so much peace," Johnnie is thinking to himself. After a couple songs the Pastor gets up and instructs the musicians to stay up there for a minute. The Pastor shares a couple testimonies of people who have recently repented of their sin and decided to follow Jesus Christ as their Savior. He shared about the new life they experienced inwardly, and the meaningful purpose they now had in life.

Johnnies thinking, "Man, I wish I had that."

Almost immediately after thinking that. The Pastor asks, "Is there anyone here tonight who may want to come forward and turn from your life of sin and follow Jesus Christ? Jesus Christ said that, *"He came so that whosoever will believe in Him shall not perish."*[11]

Johnnie's thinking, "Man I don't want to perish, I wonder what that means?"

The Pastor continues, "If there is anyone here tonight who would like to turn their life to Jesus Christ, I would ask you to come forward and allow us to pray with you."

Johnnie quickly looks at Silas and asks, "What does that mean Silas?"

"We'll Johnnie, Jesus Christ came and died on a cross for our sins. But just like if someone offers you a dollar it isn't yours unless you reach out and take it and put it in your pocket. Jesus poured out His blood so that whosoever would believe in Him will not perish but have eternal life. But we must reach out and take it by faith.

---

[11] John 3:16

Jesus loves you Johnnie. Do you want me to go up there with you?" Johnnie's heart is beating rapidly as he says, "Yes please do. I want to know more about Jesus."

Johnnie and Silas make their way up to the front of the church and the Pastor explains to Johnnie with his Bible open that, *"we have all sinned and fallen short of the glory of God.*[12] You see Johnnie, God is a Holy God and the Bible says *"that without Holiness no man will see God."*[13] "There is nothing we can do as far as good works to get to heaven and escape the lake of fire Johnnie."

He flips through the pages in his Bible and reads, *"When His disciples heard it, they were greatly astonished, saying," "Who then can be saved?" But Jesus looked at them and said to them, With men this is impossible, but with God all things are possible."* [14] "You see Johnnie *we*

---

[12] Romans 3:23
[13] Hebrews 12:14
[14] Matthew 19:25-26

are saved by Grace through faith,[15] *we must repent of our sin,*[16] and make Jesus our Savior, and our Lord. Would you like to commit your life to Him Johnnie?"

"Yes, I would Pastor, I really would, I want to learn more about Him and serve Him. You may think I am crazy, but I saw Jesus that night in the hospital and there is nothing like Him in the world. As I stand here things seem to be making a little more sense to me as far as what I have been going through. I want to know Jesus Pastor."

"Say this prayer after me Johnnie."

"Yes sir."

After saying a prayer of repentance and committing his life to the Lord, Johnnie was in a sea of peace like he has never experienced before in his entire life. As if he could literally

---

[15] Ephesians 2:8
[16] Luke 13:3

feel the weight of shame, depression and guilt leave his soul. Johnnie and Silas made their way back to where they were sitting. The worship team started again singing beautiful music unto Jesus.

Johnnie tells Silas, "I have never felt this way Silas, something wonderful happened to me up there while we were praying, something wonderful!" As the music continues Johnnie suddenly feels a river of peace flood his very soul as if he were drinking living water of *peace, love, and joy.*[17] It was as if his breath was taken from him as a new breath from heaven filled his very soul. Peace continued to fill his inward spirit like *living water to a thirsty man.*[18] Johnnie could no longer stand and had to sit down as tears of inexpressible joy ran down his face. He was repeatedly saying, I love you Jesus, I love you Jesus, thank you Jesus.[19] For the next hour and

---

[17] Nehemiah 8:10
[18] John 4:10
[19] Acts 3:19

a half this continued as the Holy Spirit continually washed into Johnnie.

Johnnie finally stands up and looks around for Silas. He makes his way into the restroom and looks in the mirror and notices that his eyes are clearer. As though he can visibly see the peace on his face. "Wow," Johnnie thinks to himself, "I never knew this kind of love and peace was possible." Johnnie walks out of the restroom inwardly saying, "Thank you Jesus, thank you Jesus." He runs into Silas.

"Hey, there you are," says Silas, "Did Jesus answer your prayer this evening?"

"Oh, absolutely Silas. I can hardly believe what He did for me in there. I want to serve Him with everything within me. Will you help me learn the Bible?"

"Absolutely Johnnie,[20] we will help each other *through the narrow gate*[21] A good Christian friend is important to help us along the way."[22]

"Man Silas, I don't feel like going home. There is so much love in this place."

"Well it is getting late Johnnie and we can meet back here on Wednesday if you'd like?"

"Oh absolutely, I will be here Silas, thank you so much for inviting me. I feel like a brand-new man."[23]

"Ha Johnnie I'm so excited for ya. You know that is exactly what the Bible says, it says, *that whoever is in Christ is a new creation and that all things have become new.*"

"Well that is how I feel Silas."

"Oh, wait Johnnie, I almost forgot. I was so excited about all that the Lord did for you

---

[20] Ecclesiastes 4:12
[21] Matthew 7:13
[22] Proverbs 27:17
[23] 2 Corinthians 5:17

tonight I almost forgot to get you a Bible. Do you have one?"

"No Silas I don't. I sure would love one though."

As they look over, they notice the Pastor coming down the hall with a big smile on his face that expressed he was full of excitement. Holding a Bible in his hand as if he knew they were talking about getting Johnnie one.

"Hey Johnnie, I'm so happy for you. I did not want you to leave tonight without this Bible. Its brand-new leather bound. It is important for you to start reading this now and allow it to bring you closer to the Lord. To help you mature in your relationship with Jesus Christ."[24]

"Thank you, Pastor it's kind of funny that you brought me this. Silas and I were just talking about getting me a Bible."[25]

---

[24] Ephesians 5:26
[25] Matthew 6:8-b

"God has done a wonderful thing for you tonight Johnnie, don't ever forget it. Make sure you start to develop a good prayer life. This will be your lifeline with the Lord.[26] And make sure you start to learn and obey all that is written in His Word, the Bible."[27]

"Yes Sir," Johnnie replied full of excitement. "I want to serve Him well."

"If you ever need anything Johnnie you make sure to call me or stop by the church, anytime okay."

"Okay, thank you Pastor."

"Ok, have a good night I have to be getting home now."

As Silas and Johnnie are leaving and walking home Johnnie says, "Man, thanks again for praying for me and all that you've done Silas."

---

[26] 1 Thessalonians 5:17
[27] Matthew 28:19

"You just keep thanking Jesus Johnnie. I am just his servant, but just so you know it is very much my pleasure. You know where I live, and I would like to exchange phone numbers with you as well if you don't mind so we can call each other. I think we should pray about you helping with the youth group. We must learn to pray about all things Johnnie."[28]

As they walk home Johnnie tells Silas, "I can hardly wait to tell Priscilla what happened to me tonight."

Silas looks at him with a grin as he says, "I remember when I first came to know Jesus and began to tell all my friends. Ha, not all of them were as excited about it as I was Johnnie."

As they approach Johnnies house Silas says, "Well Johnnie, I encourage you to read, read, and read some more of the Bible. The more Bible you get in your spirit, the stronger you'll

---

[28] Philippians 4:6

be. You will notice that it will become like food for your spirit," Silas says with a sparkle in his eyes.[29]

"Will do man, I'm going to go dive into it right now," replies Johnnie. "Have a good night Silas, I'll be seeing ya around."

"Okay Johnnie, have a good one."

Johnnie runs upstairs and jumps on his bed and starts reading in the New Testament where Pastor told him to start. Johnnie's eyes are glued in this book, "Man, Silas is right, this is like food for me." Johnnie thinks to himself. Page after page he reads passages that seem to leap off the pages at him. As he reads many passages, he remembers hearing the Pastor and Silas saying these scriptures. Not even knowing that they were quoting out of the Bible. Johnnie finally falls asleep around two o'clock in the morning.

---

[29] Matthew 4:4

Johnnie wakes up at four a.m. full of excitement and joy. He hurries and opens the Bible as it falls open Johnnie reads these words, *"Then I will give them one heart, and I will put a new spirit within them, and take the stony heart out of their flesh, and give them a heart of flesh, that they may walk in My statutes and keep My judgments and do them; and they shall be My people, and I will be their God."* [30]

"Oh God, thank You." Johnnie whispers. "I know Lord that this is what you have done for me. I want to walk in Your statutes Jesus." As Johnnie is praying, he notices the glory of the Lord filling his room where he is praying. Again, the Holy Spirit begins to wash over him and fill him with a love he has never experienced. This continues for another two hours as Johnnie is not wanting this experience to ever end. He hears his mom walking up the stairs. "Oh God,

[30] Ezekiel 11:19

would you please do this for my mom? Please help me to tell her about your love."

As he's praying, he hears his mom knocking on the door. Johnnie quickly sits up on his bed and says, "Come in."

"Good morning Johnnie, I didn't hear you come in last night. Is everything okay?"

"Yes mom, everything is great! It's never been better mom," he says with a look of inexpressible joy on his face almost as if he's illuminated.

"Well Johnnie you sure look good, you look different. What did you do last night?"

"Mom, I went to church with Silas. I was feeling so down coming home from the park and ran into Silas and decided to go to church with him. Mom, I accepted Jesus Christ as my Lord and Savior last night. He is so real mom, He's so real! I found out that it is not about religion mom. It's about coming to terms that we are separated from God because of our sin. But God loves us so much that if we repent, He will reveal Himself to us and fill our heart with His love mom. He is so wonderful."

"That's nice Johnnie, I am really happy for you. Now were you still planning on getting plugged back into school today? Remember? Today was the day you were going to return to school."

Johnnie had forgotten about returning to school, and a little saddened that his mom didn't genuinely seem very excited about his new-found faith in Jesus. "Yea mom, I'll hurry and get ready now, will you take me?"

"Yes Johnnie, I will take you," she says as she notices the new excitement and life Johnnie seems to have.

"Okay great, thanks mom, I will tell you more about Jesus tonight," he says as he runs to get cleaned up for school.

As Johnnie is in first period, he notices a kid he has seen quite a bit in school who has always seemed kind of sad and not very popular. Johnnie's heart begins to feel a lot of compassion for this kid. After the bell rings Johnnie approaches him and says, "Hey what's up man? My name is Johnnie, how are you doing today?"

"Hi Johnnie, I'm Steven, and I'm doing alright" he says with his head hung kind of low as if he isn't used to conversation.

"Well it's nice to meet you Steven. I've seen you around a lot but never got a chance to meet you."

"Yeah I've seen you around too Johnnie. You hang out with Mark and them right, and cruise around in that cool mustang?"

"Ha yea, yea I do. Hey, you're welcome to go hang out with us sometime if you want. We usually have a good time."

"Alright Johnnie sure, sounds fun."

"Well cool man, give me your number and I'll be giving you a call Steven."

As Steven writes it down and gives it to Johnnie he says, "I got to be getting to class now, have a good day Johnnie."

Chapter Five
Spiritual Gifts

As Johnnie walks away, he feels deeply grieved and sneaks outside to pray. Sitting at a table under a tree outside the School he hears the voice of the Lord say.

"Johnnie, I sent you to talk to Steven because he is contemplating suicide. Both of his parents were killed in a car accident last year. He is searching for answers, but he has not come to Me for those answers. Now is his time Johnnie. Go and tell him that the prescription medication that he is taking will only lead him down into more darkness and that I have came to set him free."

Hearing this Johnnie gets nervous and thinks to himself, "Man, won't this offend him, I wonder if anyone even knows he is taking prescription medication?" Then Johnnie remembers the Bible verse that says,

"Abraham believed God, and it was accounted to him for righteousness"[31]

Quickly followed by,

"And lean not on your own understanding; in all your ways acknowledge Him, And He shall direct your paths.[32]

Immediately after this he remembers the verse that says,

"They glorify God for the obedience of your confession to the gospel of Christ, and for your liberal sharing with them and all men"[33]

As Johnnie experiences this he answers. "Yes Lord, I will tell him please forgive me for my timidity. I said I want to serve You well, and I meant it. I will tell him."

After this Johnnie heads to his next class, arriving fifteen minutes late. As his teacher is

---

[31] Romans 4:3
[32] Proverbs 3:5-6
[33] 2 Corinthians 9:13

speaking Johnnie is so full of excitement over his experience with the Lord, he has a difficult time paying attention to what his teacher is saying. After the bell rings Johnnie quickly makes his way to Steven's locker. As Steven approaches Johnnie says, "Hey Steven, how's it going man?"

"Pretty good Johnnie, I always look forward to lunch time."

"Ha, me too," says Johnnie. "Hey Steven, can I eat lunch with ya today?" Johnnie asks kind of timidly.

"Sure Johnnie, I usually just bring a lunch and sit in the lunchroom, but you're welcome to join me."

"Great, I'm going to go get my lunch, I'll meet ya in there." Johnnie runs to his locker to get his Bible and throws it in his backpack and quickly makes his way to the lunchroom and finds Steven sitting in the back by himself. Johnnie is feeling nervous as he approaches Steven and is battling thoughts of doubt. Right before Johnnie sits down, he hears these words in his spirit,

"Behold, to obey is better than sacrifice"[34]

"Hey Johnnie," says Steven, "Where is your lunch?"

Johnnie grins saying, "well, I must have forgotten it Steven."

Johnnie takes a deep breath and says, "Steven, God sent me to tell you that He has the answers you're looking for. He loves you and has seen the pain you have experienced when you lost your parents in that car accident last year. He wants you to know that He is saddened to see you taking prescriptions to try to heal your pain and that He Himself wants to heal your pain Steven. He showed me that your parents were Christians and that they loved you very much. You rebelled against church because you felt like

---

[34] 1 Samuel 15:22

you never fit into their box. But God doesn't want to place you in a box Steven. He wants to take you out of the box you're in and set you free." After saying this Johnnie is blown away how all this just seemed to flow out of his mouth. Johnnie quickly hears these words hit his spirit,

"Do not worry beforehand, or premeditate what you will speak. But whatever is given you in that hour, speak that; for it is not you who speak, but the Holy Spirit".[35]

As Johnnie looks at Steven, he notices tears filling his eyes. Steven was shaken to the core of his being upon hearing these words.

Steven quietly asks, "Johnnie, how did you know all this?"

"Steven, I recently became a Christian and I'm telling you that God wants you to know that He loves you. He is so real Steven."

---

[35] Mark 13:11

After a minute of silence Steven says with teary eyes, "Ya know Johnnie, what you said is true. I never really felt like I fit in at church. And then when I lost my parents and had to go through the adoption process, I felt like God was mad at me because I never really got involved in church. But this must be God talking because there is no way anyone could know that I have been taking pain killers to make myself feel better to cope with this depression. I have always dreamed of doing something great for God but never have been able to believe that He would use someone like me."

As Johnnie listens to Steven his eyes are instantly opened into the spirit realm. He sees an angry ghostly image in the form of a man. Standing behind Steven holding a chain. The chain is connected to shackles on Steven's wrists and ankles. This ghostly image is wearing a sash with the name, "*suicide*" on it. Johnnie notices this angry spirit is staring right at Johnnie, expressing deep hatred for him. Johnnie being a little freaked out, tries not to flinch as he does not want Steven to know what he sees. Johnnie is filled with anger toward suicide having a stronghold on Steven. As Johnnie is being filled with strength and faith, he sees in the spirit that suicide seems to turn his expressions from rage, to fear. Suicide is starting to frantically shake and tremble. Now in the natural Steven seems to be a little teary eyed and looking as if his faith is being lifted to a new level.

Johnnie says sternly. "Steven, the devil is a liar. [36] God isn't mad at you. He came to give you life and life more abundantly. He is the Good Sheppard.[37] For He knows the thoughts He thinks toward you. He has thoughts of peace toward you Steven, thoughts to give you a future and a hope[38] and you'll find this peace when you seek Him with all your heart.[39] Steven, I

---

[36] John 8:44
[37] John 10:10-11
[38] Jeremiah 29:11
[39] Jeremiah 29:13

recently went through some very dark depression. And I can honestly say that I know what it's like. But when I received Jesus Christ as my Lord and Savior, He set me free from those chains. He can do the same for you Steven. This is not about religion, but rather about Jesus Christ and coming into terms that we are separated from Him because of our sin. And that we can come back into a right relationship with God by His grace through faith in Jesus Christ because of the sacrifice He offered for us on the cross."[40]

Immediately after saying this, the bell rang signaling them to go to their next class.

Steven looks at Johnnie and says, "I believe everything your saying Johnnie."

Once Steven said, "I believe what you're saying Johnnie,"

---

[40] Ephesians 2:8

Johnnie instantly saw a large glorious angel with a large build. The angel is holding a large shining sword. The angel's eyebrows are tipped as though he is confident and ready for battle. As this strong angel approaches toward Steven. Johnnie sees that suicide is no match for this powerful angel. Immediately suicide hurriedly removes the shackles from Steven's wrists and ankles. With a look of great fear suicide vanishes through the wall and leaves.

This angel with blond curly hair and bright blue eyes turned his head expressing strength, confidence, and a look of great victory. He says to Johnnie, "Good job, Steven is free from suicide now."

Johnnie replied, "Thank you."

With a victorious look on his face and full of joy. The angel gives Johnnie a grin and winked at him as he took off through the ceiling.

Johnnie sees all this and keeps his composure so Steven dont know.

Steven continues saying, "Man, I feel so much better just talking with you Johnnie. I would love to hear more, can we meet sometime?"

"Absolutely Steven, here is my phone number. Would you be interested in going to church with me and Silas? I'm confident you won't regret it Steven."

"Yes, said Steven, I would actually love to go."

"Okay, great man, Silas and I will pick you up at nine o clock Sunday morning, sound okay?"

"Yes, sounds good man, I'm actually looking forward to it."

"Alright man, I'm going to run to class, thanks so much for listening to me Steven, I'm excited for you and looking forward to seeing you again."

"Me too Johnnie," says Steven, "Laters man."

After this conversation Johnnie went running through the hallways with his heart pounding with excitement and joy for all that the Lord just did for Steven. Johnnie is looking for Silas so he could share the good news with him. [41] Instead he runs into Priscilla knocking her books out of her hand.

"Oh my goodness Priscilla, I'm so sorry" says Johnnie as he's picking up her books for her.

Priscilla laughs and says, "That's okay Johnnie, it's good to see ya, you look great, and why are you in such a hurry? When are we going to go out and do something together?"

"Man Priscilla, you look good too, I was just looking for Silas, how have you been?"

Priscilla says, "I've been okay, I miss you though, when are we going to go out and spend some time together?"

"Well, I don't know, maybe this weekend or something, what were you thinking?"

---

[41] Acts 15:3

"I don't know Johnnie, but I'll call you okay," as she leans up and kisses Johnnie on the cheek.

"Okay Priscilla, I've got to go," as Johnnie hurries down the hallway. Priscilla is feeling like Johnnie seemed a little uninterested for the first time in their relationship.

Johnnie finds Silas next to his locker and runs up to him with his heart pounding and full of excitement says, "Silas, you're never going to believe what just happened. I just spoke with Steven about the Lord and God gave me words to speak like never before. I was up late reading and almost got through the whole New Testament. I also studied many passages in the Old Testament. And all the scriptures that I read seemed to just flow out of my mouth, and Steven is going to go to church with us this Sunday. Man Silas, it was amazing, God is so good."

"Wow, Johnnie, the Lord is already using you. Praise God, the bible says,

"You did not choose Him, but He chose you and appointed you that you should go and bear fruit, and that your fruit should remain,"[42]

"I knew there was a calling from God on your life Johnnie, I'm so proud of you for obeying the Lord and stepping out in faith. I remember that night when you were in the hospital I had so much faith that the Lord was going to bring you back. I was shaking you like a rag doll praying for you, and you came back to life. It was weird because even after Dr Graham declared you dead. Everyone still blew it off as a coincidence. But I know the Lord raised you from the dead. Man, He is so awesome, praise God for you Johnnie."

"Man Silas, I haven't told no one yet, but I know what your saying is true, because I was in hell, and then I saw the Lord ascending out of the expanse and he came to me and said, "It's not yet your time" and then I remember Mark

---

[42] John 15:16

saying you were shaking me, and I knew it was because you were praying, Glory to God! I haven't told anyone because they may think I'm crazy, but I know you'll believe. And now Steven is going to be next to know of God's goodness."

"Amen Johnnie. I want to know more about your experience when we have more time."

"Oh man Silas, I can't wait to tell you. I don't even want to go to class. I just want to talk about the Lord, and all this school stuff seems so dead and uninteresting now."

"Tell me about it Johnnie, you're so right. Let's pray together about full time ministry for the Lord, I'm so ready to stop running this world's race, I want to run a good race for Jesus Christ. I want to say as the Apostle Paul, *"Nor do I count my life dear to myself, so that I may finish my race with joy, and the ministry which I received from the Lord Jesus, to testify to the gospel of the grace of God".*[43]

"Wow Silas, I just read that last night too, and that's what I was thinking. I also read where the Apostle Paul said,

"I have been crucified with Christ; it is no longer I who live, but Christ lives in me; and the life which I now live in the flesh I live by faith in the Son of God, who loved me and gave Himself for me."[44]

"Man Silas, I can hardly believe how all this scripture is so easy to remember."

"Wow Johnnie, God has anointed your life. It's not you remembering, its the Holy Spirit. The Bible says,

"But the Helper, the Holy Spirit, whom the Father will send in His name, He will teach you

---

[43] Acts 20:24
[44] Galatians 2:20

all things, and bring to your remembrance all things that He said to you."[45]

"Hey, I remember reading that too somewhere in John. The Bible is so cool.

"Ha, alright Johnnie, I better get to class man. Do you want to get together and go through the gospel of John tonight or something?"

"Sure Silas, let's do it, call me later, see ya."

After school Johnnie decided to take a city bus home. While on the bus his attention goes to the neighborhood around him. It seemed run down and oppressed. Johnnie feels compassion and love for the people that he sees as the bus goes through the streets.

Then he hears in his spirit, *"So Johnnie, for what purpose do you suppose I came into the world?"*

---

[45] John 14:26

Johnnie starts thinking and pulls out his Bible and as it falls open his eyes read,

"For the Son of Man has come to seek and to save that which was lost."[46]

"Wow," Johnnie thinks to himself and closes the Bible, He pauses, "Okay, I'm going to open this again." As he opens the Bible his eyes read,

"For this purpose the Son of God was manifested, that He might destroy the works of the devil."[47]

As Johnnie ponders this, he is filled with compassion for these people around him. It appears they were lost. And that the works of the devil were evident in this neighborhood. As Johnnie continues pondering all these things, he hears,

"The Spirit of the Lord is upon Me, because He has anointed Me to preach the gospel to the

---

[46] Luke 19:10
[47] 1 John 3:8

poor; He has sent Me to heal the brokenhearted, To proclaim liberty to the captives and recovery of sight to the blind, To set at liberty those who are oppressed; To proclaim the acceptable year of the Lord." [48]

"Lord, did you want me to go into these neighborhoods?" Johnnie prayed, then he heard, "*Johnnie I say unto you that,*

The harvest truly is plentiful, but the laborers are few. Therefore pray the Lord of the harvest to send out laborers into His harvest. [49]

Johnnie, would I ask you to pray, if I didn't expect you to go?"

"*Therefore Go, And as you go, preach, saying, 'The kingdom of heaven is at hand.' Heal the sick, cleanse the lepers, raise the dead, cast out demons. Freely you have received, freely give. Provide neither gold nor silver nor*

---

[48] Luke 4:18-19
[49] Matthew 9:37-38

copper in your money belts, nor bag for your journey, nor two tunics, nor sandals, nor staffs; for a worker is worthy of his food." [50]

Upon hearing this Johnnie is overcome with a compassion and desire to see these people experience the love of God.

As Johnnie is finally arriving home approaching his front door. He sees Silas just getting ready to walk away. "Oh, man Silas, I'm sorry, have you been here long? I totally forgot you was coming over tonight. I feel like the Lord was teaching me some things on the bus ride and I lost track of time."

"No Johnnie, I just got here actually, Man Johnnie, after seeing the Lord work wonders in your life, and hearing about Steven today in school. I'm sure getting a passion to share our Lord's gospel with all that I can. I've been getting these crazy ideas of doing some outreach

---

[50] Matthew 10:7-10

in some of the rougher neighborhoods around us. Its almost as if I have the faith that the Lord will,

"Stretch out His hand to heal, and that signs and wonders will be done through our Lord Jesus."[51]

Ever since you got converted Johnnie, my faith has gone through the roof. His presence has been stronger as He has led me into more prayer time. He is all I've been thinking about."

"Silas, you're not going to believe what the Lord was showing me on the bus ride home, let's go upstairs I'm going to show you these scriptures the Lord was giving me regarding these neighborhoods and His heart for the people. I believe the Lord is showing us the same things." As they get upstairs Johnnie opens his Bible and his eyes fall on,

---

[51] Acts 4:30

"Let us go into the next towns, that I may preach there also, because for this purpose I have come forth."[52]

"Oh my goodness Silas, look at this, another one. Look at all that the Lord has shown me regarding why He came. I was on the bus coming home and the Lord asked me why I thought He came into the world. Since then He has shown me these scriptures,

"For the Son of Man has come to seek and to save that which was lost"[53]

"For this purpose the Son of God was manifested, that He might destroy the works of the devil,"[54]

"Let us go into the next towns, that I may preach there also, because for this purpose I have come forth."[55]

---

[52] Mark 1:38
[53] Luke 19:10
[54] 1John 3:8
[55] Mark 1:38

And then He showed me the reason that the Holy Spirit was upon Him so that He could, *"preach the gospel to the poor; to heal the brokenhearted, to proclaim liberty to the captives and recovery of sight to the blind, to set at liberty those who are oppressed*; and to *proclaim the acceptable year of the Lord"* [56]

"It seems pretty evident to me Silas why He came. And then He asked me why we're supposed to pray to the Lord to send the harvesters if He didn't want me to go?"

"Hey Johnnie, it's a real blessing to be able to hang around such a young Christian who's full of God's Spirit. Because you haven't been indoctrinated by man's gospel. I encourage you to stay in His Word and allow Him to teach you. Look at this scripture,"

"But the anointing which you have received from Him abides in you, and you do not need

---

[56] Luke 4:18-19

that anyone teach you; but as the same anointing teaches you concerning all things, and is true, and is not a lie, and just as it has taught you, you will abide in Him"[57]

"The Lord's teaching you Johnnie. *"Blessed are you, for flesh and blood has not revealed this to you, but God who is in heaven.*[58]

"And how wonderful it is. Make sure you always stay close to your Teacher.

"That's good stuff Silas, I will, thank you."

"Your welcome Johnnie and your correct in regard of why He came, for it is written that, *"This is a faithful saying and worthy of all acceptance, that Christ Jesus came into the world to save sinners!* [59]

"Wow, replied Johnnie, with all these scriptures, how can we doubt?

---

[57] 1 John 2:27
[58] Matthew 16:17
[59] 1 Timothy 1:15

Chapter six
The Wilderness

They spent three hours in prayer and time reading scripture and drawing near to the Lord. Then Silas says, "Well I better get going home now Johnnie. Man, what a great time I had tonight."

"Yeah me-too Silas. Remember to keep Steven in your prayers. I just know that he is going to experience God's amazing grace. I'm excited for him."

"Amen, me too Johnnie, I will definitely be praying for him, we'll see ya in the a.m. hour."

"Alright man, have a good night."

The next morning Johnnie awakes and starts off in prayer and time drawing near to the Lord. An hour passes and Johnnie prays, "Lord, where is your presence this morning? It appears my prayers are hitting the ceiling and bouncing back down to me. Where are you Lord? I cannot feel your wonderful presence." Johnnie opens his Bible and finds himself in Psalms as he reads,

"Where can I go from Your Spirit? Or where can I flee from Your presence? If I ascend into heaven, You are there; If I make my bed in hell, behold, You are there. If I take the wings of the morning, And dwell in the uttermost parts of the sea, Even there Your hand shall lead me, And Your right hand shall hold me.[60]

"Well alright Lord, I know you're with me." Johnnie runs down the stairs as his mom is making him breakfast.

"Hey, good morning Johnnie, how did you sleep?"

"Oh, I slept real good mom, you?"

---

[60] Psalm 139:7-10

"I did too Johnnie." As they are sitting down at the breakfast table enjoying breakfast, they hear loud music and the sound of Mark's pipes screaming out of the back of his muscle car as he pulls in the driveway.

Johnnie gets up to let Mark in and notices that Priscilla is with him.

"Hey, was up? Johnnie be good," Mark says as usual.

"Hey Mark, Priscilla, come on in. Good to see you all, come get some breakfast," Johnnie says with a genuine smile and a fresh twinkle in his eyes.

Priscilla says, "Johnnie, you sure look good. I'm sure glad to see you looking so happy."

"Yeah Johnnie, you do look a little different," says Mark.

"Ha, you guys know what. I surrendered my life to Jesus Christ. He is so real. All I have ever heard about before is religion. I never knew that

Jesus Christ could be so real in someone's life, or I would have done this a long time ago."

"Oh cool," says Mark as he rolls his eyes at Priscilla as if Johnnie is losing it.

Johnnie sees this and says, "Hey you guys I'm really sorry but I'm going to take the bus to school today. I hope that doesn't upset you."

"You mean like, the city bus?" Asks Priscilla.

"Yeah I took it home yesterday and I actually enjoyed it. I know, sounds kind of crazy huh." Johnnie says with a grin.

"Yeah, it kind of does," says Mark as he puts down his bagel and walks out the door saying, "C'mon Priscilla, I don't want to be late."

"Oh, I'm going to take the bus with Johnnie. I mean, if that's okay with you Johnnie?"

"Oh absolutely Priscilla, you sure you want to take the bus?"

"Yeah, it'll be fun. We'll see ya later Mark, have a good day," Priscilla says kind of rudely because she didn't like Mark's response toward Johnnies testimony.

As Mark leaves Priscilla says, "Wow, that was kind of awkward. What is Mark's problem? Remember Johnnie I told you a couple weeks ago on your couch that I don't care if you join a religion. I just wanted to be with you? Well, I meant it."

When hearing this Johnnies heart is overcome with a deep love for Priscilla. Then, to spoil the moment Johnnie's mom who is standing behind Priscilla gives Johnnie a thumbs up and winks with a big silly smile on her face. Expressing that Johnnie is the luckiest guy in the world to find a girl that seems so faithful. Johnnie responds with a grin and tries not to laugh at his mom in the background. Priscilla quickly turns around and sees his mom with her thumb up and big goofy grin. As Priscillas face turns a little red she turns back to Johnnie with a big smile on her face.

As Johnnie and Priscilla go out to catch the bus, they notice it looks as though they may get a good rain storm. When they get on the bus the rain begins to poor down. The clouds are so thick the sky is dark as if it is nighttime.

Priscilla asks, "So Johnnie, why did ya start taking the bus to school?"

"I don't know Priscilla, but on my way home yesterday I really felt like I wanted to do something for some of these neighborhoods. Maybe try to make a positive impact on the community."

"Wow Johnnie, that actually sounds pretty cool, but don't people who are older usually do those kinds of things?"

"Yeah, I suppose your right Priscilla, but I'm about to change that." He says with a determined look of confidence.

"Ha," Priscilla laughs. "Well, what are we going to do for a positive impact?"

"I don't know yet Priscilla, that's why I'm coming through on the bus to get some ideas together. Many of these little kids have fathers in prison and mother's hooked on drugs. Many of their families are gang members. Could you imagine the brokenness of these kids who need someone to spend time with them?"

"Well I guess I never thought of it Johnnie. Your right, it's kind of sad."

"It is Priscilla. God loves them. And He wants to show them His love, and I want to bring His love to them."

"I should have known it was this new-found religion putting you up to this. What religion are you doing this for?" Asks Priscilla.

"It's not for a religion Priscilla, the bible says,

"Delight yourself also in the Lord, And He shall give you the desires of your heart".[61]

It is the Lord who is giving me these idea's Priscilla."

Upon arriving at school, the rain is at a steady down pour. They notice that classes for the day have been cancelled due to flooding in the electrical room.

"Oh bummer," laughs Priscilla, "I guess we'll have to go hang out at your house and play some video games."

"Ha, let's get on that outbound bus," laughs Johnnie.

As they are squeezing the water from their clothes on the bus trying to dry off Johnnie says sarcastically, "Hey, do you want to know the good news Priscilla? This bus drops us off a

---

[61] Psalm 37:4

block from my house. And on top of that, my mom isn't home to let us in and I forgot my key."

"Woohoo" laughs Priscilla.

"But no worries," says Johnnie, "I can get in the window." They finally arrive at their stop. They decide they are going to sprint to Johnnie's house to try to stay dry. But by the time they're less than halfway they are totally soaked and figure they may as well walk. Arriving at the house Johnnie manipulates a window and gets in and opens the door for Priscilla.

Priscilla comes in laughing saying, "Well that was fun."

"Oh yeah, what a blast," laughs Johnnie. Johnnie turns around to hang up his jacket and Priscilla grabs his cheeks with her hands and slowly leans up and starts to kiss Johnnie.

With a serious look on her face she says, "I love you Johnnie. I want to spend the rest of my life with you," as she starts kissing him again.

"Were all alone Johnnie, let's go up into your room," as she is passionately kissing him.

Johnnie's heart is beating fast as Priscilla is driving him crazy. He stops her and puts his hands on her cheeks and softly whispers, "Priscilla, I can't. Please don't be mad at me, I'm crazy about you. But I can't be intimate until I'm married. Trust me Priscilla, this isn't easy. But it's the right thing to do."

Priscilla ignores him and presses up against him kissing him and running her fingers through his hair, "C'mon Johnnie, were in love with each other, it'll be okay. Let's go upstairs Johnnie."

Priscilla, "Stop it, you're driving me crazy, and I mean it, I can't do this."

Priscilla laughs and continues to kiss him as she is grinning.

Johnnie says, "Stop Priscilla, please." As he walks away and sits on the couch and turns on the television.

Priscilla looks upset, feeling embarrassed, rejected, and hurt. She runs out the door crying and heads up the street running in the rain.

Johnnie runs out on the porch yelling "Priscilla, get back here, Priscilla, c'mon. Don't be mad at me. I love you Priscilla"

Priscilla keeps running without looking back. Johnnie goes back and sits on the couch and begins to channel surf.

"Man, what a day, prayer time seemed dry this morning, Mark doesn't like me anymore and now Priscilla is pissed off at me. On top of that I'm soaking wet." Johnnie picks up his bible and continues reading for the next five hours. As Johnnie is reading, he comes across this passage,

"No temptation has overtaken you except such as is common to man; but God is faithful, who will not allow you to be tempted beyond what you are able, but with the temptation will also make the way of escape, that you may be able to bear it. [62]

"Man," Johnnie thinks to himself. "That seemed close to being more temptation than I could bear. And on top of that I feel as though I'm losing all my friends."

The next day Johnnie arrives at school and is looking for Silas. As he approaches his locker, he notices that the school police are going through it.

"Hey, what are you guys doing?" Asks Johnnie.

"Young man, is this your locker?" Asks the police.

"Yes it is, is there a problem officer?"

---

[62] 1 Corinthians 10:13

"Young man, please turn around and place your hands against the wall. Your being placed under arrest for possession of cocaine with the intent to sale."

"What? I've never done or sold drugs in my life, what the heck are you talking about?"

"Well, can you explain how this cocaine got into your locker?"

"No, No I can't. But I assure you it is not mine." Johnnie notices that there is a crowd of kids watching this go down. Realizing his reputation is ruined he is feeling extremely embarrassed and ashamed.

Silas walks up and says, "Hey, what is going on officer?"

"Silas, I didn't do anything man, honest, you have got to believe me." Johnnie says with tears coming down his face.

"I do believe you Johnnie. I'll be here for you. don't worry, we will get it all straightened out."

The police bring Johnnie out to their car as the kids in school are all laughing at him.

Arriving at the police station the police are calling his mom explaining to her that Johnnie has just been caught with five ounces of cocaine wrapped up for distribution. And that he will be facing felony charges and looking at doing time in the county jail.

"Oh, my gosh officer, don't you need proof that those are my drugs? I have never been in trouble with the law before. Are you guy's crazy? What in the world is going on?"

The officer says, "Well young man, the drugs were in your locker. As far as the school records show you are not sharing your locker with anyone. And you told us yourself that you are not sharing your locker with anyone. The drugs were in your possession. This pretty much tells us that they are yours. Now please Johnnie, step over here so we can get your fingerprints."

After Johnnie is stripped down and given a new orange jump suit for a wardrobe. He is placed in a cell with seven other inmates who do not seem like very nice people. Johnnie is scared to death. He immediately goes into prayer quietly within his heart.

"God, I thank You that,

"*No weapon formed against me shall prosper,*"[63]

And that even,

"*though I walk through the valley of the shadow of death, I will fear no evil; for You are with me; Your rod and Your staff, they comfort me. You prepare a table before me in the presence of my enemies; You anoint my head with oil; my cup runs over. Surely goodness and mercy shall follow me all the days of my*

---

[63] Isaiah 54:17

133

life; and I will dwell in the house of the Lord Forever".[64]

And God I thank You that,

"You have not given me a spirit of fear, but of power and of love and of a sound mind."[65]

"In God I have put my trust; I will not be afraid. What can man do to me?"[66]

While Johnnie is praying, he is interrupted.

"Hey man, what you in for, what did you do hold up a liquor store or something?" Someone asks sarcastically. The jail cell fell silent, then suddenly all the others in the cell began to laugh. One of the other inmates laughingly says, "No man, he probably beat up his mom or something, what'd you do man?"

---

[64] Psalm 23:4-6
[65] 2 Timothy 1:7
[66] Psalm 56:11

Johnnie answered, "Somebody at school placed some cocaine in my locker, and they think it is mine."

After saying this there is another brief moment of silence. And then all the sudden, all the inmates start laughing simultaneously. They are laughing so hard they are rolling on the jail cell floor holding their stomachs.

One of them yells as he is laughing uncontrollably, "Officer, it wasn't mine, honest officer," as he laughs even louder, they all seem to be enjoying Johnnie's time of difficulty.

Another man laughing on the bench yells, "Man officer, someone must have broken into my locker and put that cocaine in their".

As they are all laughing hysterically, one of the jail guards hits the door and says, "Johnnie, come with me, you have a visitor."

Johnnie is then taken down a long hall and through five sets of automatic doors which seem to slam behind him every time he goes through them. He finally sees his mom, Silas, and Pastor Timothy on the other side of a thick glass window. Johnnie is overcome with emotions of excitement to see them while also feeling shameful, for being in jail.

"Man, I wonder if they think I'm guilty of this?" Johnnie thinks to himself.

As Johnnie picks up the little phone next to the glass his mom says, "Johnnie, are you doing okay?"

"Oh yea mom, I'm freaking great." Johnnie says sarcastically.

"Johnnie, don't you talk to me that way!" snaps his mom. I'm here to see what is going on and to help in any way I can."

"Yes mom, I'm sorry, I'm just really frustrated." As tears begin to flow down Johnnies face.

"Johnnie, how in the world did all this cocaine get into your locker?"

"Mom, I don't know. This is crazy, I don't know."

"Johnnie the attorney said you may be looking at five years of prison time for this. Now you must have a better answer than, I don't know."

"Five years, what the heck! I didn't even do anything Mom, let me talk to Silas."

Johnnies mom hands the phone to Silas. "Johnnie, I know your innocent man and God Almighty is on your side. I cannot imagine what you're going through, and I can't say I understand why you're going through it. But I want you to know that I know that you are innocent. And I will be praying and believing God to expose the truth of this situation. Do not lose your faith Johnnie. God is faithful. You are not going to do five years in prison."

Johnnie's mom gets back on the phone and says, "Johnnie, were going to meet with the attorney tomorrow. The jailer said he would come and get you so we can talk again." At this they hear, "Times up."

"Mom, hurry, please put Pastor Timothy on the phone." The Pastor hurries and grabs the phone. Johnnie asks, "Pastor, can you please get me a Bible to read in this place?"

"Yes Johnnie, I will talk to the guards for you. Johnnie, listen to me. I know without a doubt that the Lord has a plan for your life. Remember, it's not about you. It's about you submitting to His will for your life. He is surely with you Johnnie. I want you to study out Joseph in the Old Testament. And make sure you stay in the Bible as much as you can okay. We will be praying for you every morning and evening and believing for your quick release. We must say as the Lord did in the garden, "*nevertheless not My will, but Yours, be done.*"[67]

Johnnie, remember. You didn't join a religion, you joined the Lord's military. This is the real thing. He has called you. I know this seems hard but remember to

"*Trust in the Lord with all your heart, And lean not on your own understanding; In all your ways acknowledge Him, And He shall direct your paths.*"[68]

At this the guard comes and takes the phone from Johnnie and says rudely, "I told you, times up"

Johnnie's eyes are teared up and he is worried about the other guys seeing him crying. As they head back to the cell Johnnie is wiping away his tears.

---

[67] Luke 22:42
[68] Proverbs 3:5-6

As they get back to the cell another officer yells to the guard that is moving Johnnie, "Hey, they just moved him to P.C."

"What is P.C.?" Johnnie asks the guard.

"P.C. stands for protective custody, and it means you get a cell all to yourself." Johnnie is greatly relieved from no longer having to be locked up with the other inmates.

As Johnnie enters his new four by six cell equipped with a metal toilet and sink. He lays on the bed thinking, "What the heck am I going through Lord, why is this happening?" Evening time rolls around, and the inmates seem to quiet down a little bit. Johnnie is just lying on his bed and hears a thud next to his door. As he looks up, he sees the guard kicking a paperback Bible under the steel bars towards his bed.

The guard says, "Your Pastor asked me to get this for you."

As Johnnie reaches over and grabs the Bible. He looks on the back with the outline of the book, and just at the site of the disciple's names Johnnie's eyes tear up. He now realizes how much he loves the Bible. He holds it to his chest weeping, so grateful to have it. He waits for his eyes to dry out so he can read it. Johnnie reads all night huddled up next to the cell door so he can get a little light from the hallway to shine on the pages of his Bible.

Chapter Seven

Graduation from School of the Prophets

For six long months the attorney worked. Trying to produce any evidence of Johnnie's innocence.

One morning Johnnie gets a surprise visit from his mom and his attorney. As Johnnie approaches the familiar glass window, he has been forced to visit his friends with for the last six months. He sees his mom. She has a grin of excitement and new sense of hope in her eyes.

Johnnie is thinking, "She looks like she has good news." He picks up the phone with much curiosity.

His mom says, "Johnnie, great news! Two gang members were arrested at your school and one of them openly admitted to placing those drugs into your locker."

"Mom, are you serious? Oh my gosh, Praise the Lord. What does this mean? Am I going home today?"

"Johnnie, your attorney says it may take a few days, but it looks like this thing is almost over," as tears of relief stream down her face and emotions overtake Johnnie's mom. Johnnie is filled with excitement and asked if Silas has heard the news.

"I am not sure if he has or not Johnnie, but I know Priscilla has. She is the one who came over to tell me. She really misses you Johnnie."

"Mom, I'm so excited, thank you for the help with the Bible degrees I was able to get online in here. This time was tough but not wasted. I can hardly wait to get out of here though."

After a few days pass, Johnnie is released from jail with all charges dropped and his record cleared. Johnnie hurriedly runs to see Silas to share with him all the good news.

"Johnnie, it's great to see you man. Johnnie, remember Steven from school? He is on fire for the Lord man, he has been a powerful witness for Jesus. He has been helping a lot at the youth services. It's cool because every time he shares his testimony, he shares of how you witnessed to him in the lunchroom and how God moved on his heart."

"Praise God Silas, that is so exciting. Hey Silas, I finally finished those two degrees in Biblical studies I told you about that I was studying. If you ever get married, I can marry you," Johnnie says laughingly. "But in all seriousness Silas, the one scripture I have been hanging onto is this, *"And we know that all things work together for good to those who love God, to those who are the called according to His purpose."*[69]

"The enemy tried so hard to make me doubt Silas. I cannot explain how difficult it was in

---

[69] Romans 8:28

there. But especially looking back now I can see how the Lord gave me the time to not only overcome fears and learn to trust in Him. But also, all the time I had in His Word."

"Praise God Johnnie," says Silas. "Hey, do you want to preach tonight Johnnie? Steven and I have been hitting the streets and inviting people to come. We are sure that there will be quite a few kids there that don't yet know the Lord."

"Yeah Silas, I'd love to man."

They arrive at the youth meeting an hour early to pray and prepare. They sensed an unusually strong presence of the Lord in there with them that evening.

"Man Johnnie, God is going to save some souls tonight, I can feel His presence like I haven't in a long time."

"Amen Silas, where is Steven?" Asks Johnnie.

"He has been driving the bus for us Johnnie. They should be here any second."

Steven comes walking in the door with about seventy kids from the neighborhoods. When he sees Johnnie, he runs over to him and gives him a hug saying, "Johnnie, thank you for serving the Lord man, He has set me free."

Johnnie replies, "Man Steven, what a blessing to see you on fire for Jesus Christ. Let's serve Him well together Steven, let's serve Him well."

"Amen," replies Steven, "look at all these kids from the neighborhoods He has brought in tonight. Silas told me you were preaching Johnnie, I'm excited. What are you going to preach on?"

"Well, I don't know yet Steven, I don't know."

As worship starts Johnnie is filled with compassion from Heaven for these kids. He notices the Lord giving him a fresh outpouring of the Holy Spirit for the message he is about to deliver. "Lord, what do you want me to preach tonight?" Prays Johnnie'

The Lord said, *"Johnnie, do not worry about what you will say! I have raised you up for this purpose, to preach my Word."*

After an hour of worship time Johnnie jumps up and grabs the microphone and starts out with,

"I want everybody in this room to know that Jesus Christ loves you. I know firsthand that heaven is real, and hell is real. I died in a hospital less than a year ago, I was not a Christian at this time. When I died demons came and took me to hell. I'm telling you that the horror and terror in that place is worse than anything you can imagine. I saw millions of people there screaming in pain and in torment from the fire and the demons that were attacking them. This place was a place where people will never' ever, experience a moment of quiet. There is absolutely no love, no peace, no kindness and no pity. Nor any kind of friendship in hell. Friends please hear me and hear me well tonight. Jesus Christ mentioned hell more than He mentioned heaven in the Bible, He said,

"If your right eye causes you to sin, pluck it out and cast it from you; for it is more profitable for you that one of your members perish, than for your whole body to be cast into hell. And if your right hand causes you to sin, cut it off and cast it from you; for it is more profitable for you that one of your members perish, than for your whole body to be cast into hell."[70]

"Friends, I don't know how many of you in this room have heard the Gospel before. But I want to tell you that I just spent the last six months in jail. I have heard many preachers. And I need to tell you that there is alot more to the gospel than getting rich, or getting material possessions, or anything that this world has to offer. As a matter of fact, Jesus Christ said, *"For*

---

[70] Matthew 5:29-30

after all these things the Gentiles or the pagans seek" [71]

"I have met many people in jail who have halfheartedly given their life to the Lordship of Jesus Christ. You see, they want a Savior, but they do not want a Lord.

And you precious people need someone here to tell you the truth. This is not about a religion, this is not about joining a club, and this is not about your best life now. This is about a Holy God, Jesus Christ. Who came down from Heaven, and took the punishment for our sin upon Himself so that we may be saved from the fires of hell. And live eternally in peace, in Heaven with Jesus Christ."

Johnnie pauses for a moment when he realizes he is standing on a chair on the platform. He is sweating and as he looks across the crowd. He is then aware that every eye in this place is

---

[71] Matthew 6:32

focused directly on him. "You could hear a pin drop in here," Johnnie thinks to himself. As he looks closer, he notices that almost every eye in the place is full of tears.

Johnnie gets down off the chair as he continues with a softer voice, "You guys, the Bible says that *"we have all sinned and fallen short of God's glory,*[72] the Bible also says that, *"The wages of sin is death"*[73] And that, *"without holiness, no man will see God!*[74] Friends the Bible says that, *"all liars shall have their part in the lake which burns with fire and brimstone,*[75]

Friends hear me tonight. We sometimes think that hell is only for murderers and rapist, but I'm here to tell you that if you have ever told one lie. You will spend eternity in hell forever and ever. Friends think about it. Whoever goes there, after a thousand years of extreme

---

[72] Romans 3:23
[73] Romans 6:23
[74] Hebrews 12:14
[75] Revelation 21:8

torment, you will not have even begun the time you will be there for. It is eternal, Forever.

Now who here tonight can honestly say you have never sinned, lied, or cheated on a test? Friends, none of us can." As Johnnie hesitates a few seconds.   He notices that all eyes are watching him closely. They are waiting in hope that there is a way of escape. When he knows he has their full attention, he continues and says, "Jesus Christ said,

"*unless you repent you will all likewise perish.*"[76]

"As I have told you before. I know firsthand that hell is for real. And I also know firsthand that the Bible says,"

"*For You, Lord, are good, and ready to forgive, and abundant in mercy to all those who call upon You.*" [77]

---

[76] Luke 13:3
[77] Psalm 86:5

"I want everyone within the sound of my voice to listen very, very carefully," as Johnnie tones it down a bit with a very serious look on his face he notices these kids are hanging on to every word he is saying. As he continues preaching Johnnie says,

"The Bible is clear that, *"For God so loved the world that He gave His only begotten Son, that whoever believes in Him should not perish but have everlasting life."*[78] You guys, God did not come to condemn you.[79] I want everyone to open their Bibles with me to 2 Peter 3:9, Let me read that, *"The Lord is not slack concerning His promise, as some count slackness, but is longsuffering toward us, not willing that any should perish but that all should come to repentance."*

After reading this Johnnie says, "Now flip over to Numbers 23:19, Johnnie reads,

---

[78] John 3:16
[79] John 3:17

"God is not a man, that He should lie, Nor a son of man, that He should repent. Has He said, and will He not do? Or has He spoken, and will He not make it good?"

"God is so good. He sent Jesus Christ into this world to save us, and to give us new life. I want you all to stand to your feet, listen to me. Jesus Christ can set you free. He has come to make you, *"the light of the world, a city on a hill that cannot be hidden"*[80] He will make you a wise servant who wins souls, [81] Jesus Christ said, *"Follow Me, and I will make you fishers of men."*[82] He will fill your hearts with joy, and with the Holy Spirit[83]

"If there is anyone here tonight who wants to repent of their sins. I promise you that God Almighty will forgive you. As a matter of fact, Jesus Christ said, *"Likewise, I say to you, there*

---

[80] Matthew 5:14
[81] Proverbs 11:30
[82] Matthew 4:19
[83] Acts 13:52

is joy in the presence of the angels of God over one sinner who repents."[84]

"If you are ready for a complete change of lifestyle, and to totally surrender your life to the lordship of Jesus Christ. I want you to come up here to the front and allow Silas, Steven or myself to pray with you."

At this, every kid in that place made their way to the front of the auditorium. All the kids were repenting of their sins and asking God to forgive them, the glory of the Lord filled the place. God poured out His Spirit on all of that were there.[85]

As Johnnie looked over at Silas who was praying for a young man, he noticed the young man he was praying for started yelling, "I can see out of my right eye, I can see out of my right eye!"

Johnnie walks over there and gives the young man the microphone. He asks him to tell

---

[84] Luke 15:10
[85] Acts 2:17

everybody what the Lord just did for him. While the young man is telling the crowd that he can now see out of both eyes and praising Jesus.

Silas tells Johnnie, "His eye was totally gray when I was praying for him. Look at it, his eye turned the same color brown as his other eye when we were praying."

The young man shared with everyone in awe and amazement how Jesus Christ restored his sight.

All the kids were testifying of God's amazing love in that building until three in the morning. Silas decided to just keep the building open all night and allow these teenagers to sleep there if they wanted. Almost half of them stayed all night. The next morning the worship team decided to start the day off with prayer and worship time. The kids stayed all day seeking the Lord in prayer and taking turns sharing their testimony of what the Lord had done for them. Throughout the day the kids who had to leave the previous night came back and were drawn into prayer as the presence of the Lord was resting in that building with the kids.

As evening time came Steven approached the stage and declared a fast. And asked the kids if they would join him in prayer for this revival to spread throughout Los Angeles. While these teenagers sought the Lord in prayer the Holy Spirit continued to pour over them.

Silas finally got ahold of Pastor Timothy and told him all that the Lord was doing. Silas asked him to help with the discipleship process of all these new converts. They started doing Bible studies and praying and fasting together daily. The news was quickly spreading throughout the whole city.

Some of the church members wanted to bring in cameras so they could record the services and show everyone what God was doing among the youth in Los Angeles.

Johnnie stood up and prophesied, "If you start recording these services. You will lose this revival. This is not a showcase for the saints. This is not for us to bring in worldly possessions and to make a financial reward. The glory of the Lord is our reward. For it is written, *"Blessed is the glory of the Lord from His place!"*[86]

This is about, *"denying our selves, taking up our crosses and following him."*[87] This is about, *us losing our life for His sake.*[88] This is about, *us decreasing, and Him increasing.*[89] Have we not learned? *"that no flesh should glory in His presence.*[90] And that even Jesus Christ, *"made Himself of no reputation,"*[91]

"You guys please. I learned this from studying revivals of old and watching a lot of American Christianity on television in jail. They seemed

---

[86] Ezekiel 3:12
[87] Mark 8:34
[88] Mark 8:35
[89] John 3:30
[90] 1 Corinthians 1:29
[91] Philippians 2:7

to have a form of godliness but denied its power.[92] I'm not trying to be critical, and I did see a lot of good stuff on television. But I also saw a lot of leaven. And Jesus Christ said,

"Take heed and beware of the leaven of the Pharisees and the Sadducees."[93] The Apostle Paul said,

"Your glorying is not good. Do you not know that a little leaven leavens the whole lump?"[94]

Let's not turn this into a circus. This is not a place to sale sermons or prayers. We have over 100 kids who no longer even look forward to eating food or playing video games. All they want to do is share with their neighbors and loved ones all that Jesus Christ has done for them. God will advertise this revival. Let's say as the Apostle Paul said,

---

[92] 2 Timothy 3:5
[93] Matthew 16:6
[94] 1 Corinthians 5:6

"I have been crucified with Christ; it is no longer I who live, but Christ lives in me; and the life which I now live in the flesh I live by faith in the Son of God, who loved me and gave Himself for me" [95]

The Pastor agreeing said, "Johnnie is right. No cameras or circus acts. Let's just make this a house of prayer and allow the Holy Spirit to do what He came to do. And allow God to advertise how He wants too."

They all came together and prayed together earnestly for unity and love between the saints. Many of the youth that had just given their lives to the Lord were speaking in tongues and prophesying. Many of them were homeless and were able to find food and shelter at the church building. They prayed and sought the Lord together daily in prayer.

---

[95] Galatians 2:20

Chapter Eight
Revival Fire Spreads

One morning Johnnie walks outside the church building to go meet with Steven to do some witnessing. Approaching the parking lot, he notices the local news station doing a story about the church.

Johnnie turns to go in the other direction and the Lord says to him, *"Johnnie, what are you afraid of? Go ahead and walk over there."*

Johnnie walks by the news camera and is stopped by the women who is doing the story. "Excuse me young man, we are here doing a live story about this church. We have heard that there is quite a bit of brain washing going on in here. We have heard reports of kids not even returning home. Why are so many youths talking about this place so much? And hanging out here for so many hours?"

Johnnie, *filled with the Holy Spirit* says, "Mam, when you were twelve years old you walked into a church with your aunt Michelle. The pastor told you that you were going to lead a women's ministry when you got older. But you did not believe. Because you felt insecure."

"And then on your sixteenth birthday you were alone watching television and the preacher was praying and called out your name and said, "God is calling you into women's ministry!"

"So, I ask you today lady. How long will you disobey and run from the Lord?"

At this the lady is in awe knowing every word Johnnie just spoke is true. Being shook to her core as her whole countenance changes, she asks with a troubled voice, "What must I do?[96]

"What's your name mam?" Johnnie asks.

---

[96] Acts 16:30

"My name is Lydia," as Lydia starts to cry out, "Lord thank you, Lord thank you,"

Johnnie says, "Lydia, you are being filled with the Holy Spirit." Johnnie does not even notice that the television crew is recording this live on the local news.

Lydia turns to the rest of her crew and says, "Sorry you guys, I quit. I am going to serve the Lord for the rest of my days. Young man, can you introduce me to your Pastor?"

"Oh absolutely Lydia, come with me," Johnnie says as he is full of joy and praising God for all that He has done.

Johnnie introduces Lydia to Pastor Timothy. Then he approaches the sanctuary where he sees Silas.

Silas says, "Hey Johnnie, this is amazing isn't it."

"I'm totally in awe over all that the Lord is doing Silas."

"Hey Johnnie, I was going to ask you why you preached on hell so heavy in there last week?"

"Man, I don't know Silas, to be honest I preached a few times in jail and that never came out. I have been praying about it though. And the only thing I can come up with is maybe I had to scare the hell out of them to make room for heaven to move in. To be honest Silas it scares me a little. But I wasn't expecting all that to come out of my mouth. Since then I have studied a little and found the Bible says that, *"by the fear of the Lord one departs from evil."*[97] And that,

"but others save with fear, pulling them out of the fire, hating even the garment defiled by the flesh." [98]

"I know *it's the goodness of God which leads us to repentance*[99] I have just seen a lot of people

---

[97] Proverbs 16:6
[98] Jude 23
[99] Romans 2:4

in jail giving their life to Jesus hoping to get out of jail. Or believing God to give them a lot of money when they get out. And I have never seen much repentance Silas. And salvation cannot come without repentance, Jesus said,

"Repent, and believe in the gospel."[100]

"From my experience Silas I have seen more fruit from people coming to Jesus Christ understanding their need for a Savior rather than just looking for worldly possessions. But to be honest I did not even know what I was going to preach that night, but I am convinced that it was the Lord's will for that evening. These kids are on fire man."

"Oh, no doubt about that Johnnie, I was not asking you because I doubted that. I thought it was awesome, and it scared me too." Silas says with a grin.

---

[100] Mark 1:15

"You know it's funny, the Lord, while he was in His earthly ministry, He often spoke to people according to where they were at spiritually. I don't think we can put a systematic preaching system down on this. We just need to be determined to be led by the Holy Spirit."

"Amen to that Johnnie."

Johnnie looks surprised as he sees Priscilla coming in the church sanctuary, "Hey Priscilla, how have you been doing," asks Johnnie?

"Hey Johnnie, I haven't seen you for a while. I came to apologize for running away that day at your house."

"Oh Priscilla, I am not mad at you at all."

"Johnnie, while you were in jail. I started to read the Bible alot, and I too asked Jesus Christ to be my Lord and Savior. And that night you were preaching I was hiding in the back. And I now understand your convictions that you have regarding holiness. And I want you to know that

I totally respect that. And I too want to be on that narrow path Johnnie." As Priscilla looks Johnnie directly in the eyes, straight faced and says, "Johnnie, will you marry me?"

Johnnie thinks to himself as his heart leaps with love and excitement, "Man I love this girl." He then gets a huge grin and asks, "Are you serious Priscilla? You're not supposed to ask me. The man is supposed to ask the girl to marry him."

Priscilla gives half a laugh, though expressing a deep love with teary eyes directed right at Johnnie and says, "I know that Johnnie, but we've never really been normal, have we?"

"This is true Priscilla" as Johnnie cannot seem to stop grinning and staring right back into Priscillas eyes. He continues and says, "Priscilla I must tell you. I have moved into the church building and I'm going to be studying the Bible, ministry and I'm not planning on getting a secular education or employment. So, as you pray about this you need to understand that I may not be able to provide you with very many things."

"Johnnie, I too love the Lord. And if this is His will, I am ready to give all that up. I want to serve Him well Johnnie."

Johnnie instantly remembers saying the same thing when he became a Christian, and says, "Well Priscilla, let's go pray together with the others and see what the Lord does with this. I love you so much Priscilla. I want us to talk to the Pastor and get some counseling and direction on this."

As they are heading out to pray, they notice that the parking lot is packed full of cars and people. Johnnie and Priscilla run into the youth hall and discover that it is standing room only. And that many kids are outside wanting to get in. Johnnie looks out on the street and notices three different news stations with reporters outside doing stories about the church.

Pastor Timothy walks by and grabs Johnnie by the arm and says, "Come on, were going to meet with Silas and Steven in my office."

Johnnie quickly and firmly grabs hold of Priscilla's hand and takes her with him through the crowd.

They all gather in the office as the Pastor says, "Look you guys, the Lord has heavily placed it on my heart that we must walk in holiness and purity. This is going to be huge, and as I have studied revivals of the past it seems the most critical issue has always seemed to be love, unity and holiness. We must create an atmosphere within this small group and with the other leaders of this church where we can discuss differences freely without getting angry," *"for anger gives a foothold to the devil."*[101]

"Amen Pastor" says Silas, "I am so full of love I feel as though I cannot contain it"

---

[101] Ephesians 4:27 NLT

"Praise the Lord Silas. Don't contain it. Let it run over," the Pastor says with a big grin. Pastor continues, "We will call a few meetings a week with our leadership to keep the enemy out."

Pastor looks at Johnnie and asks, "Who is this young lady?"

"Pastor Timothy, this is Priscilla, and she just asked me to marry her." Johnnie says with a big grin. With Priscillas face turning bright red she elbows Johnnie in the ribs.

Pastor grins saying, "You all must fight to keep your relationship pure. I want to talk with you two more on this when we have more time okay."

"Yes Pastor, we want that as well. I promise you we are both totally determined to keep this pure and to serve Jesus well."

"Well alright then, we have three news stations out front. Many neighborhoods in Los Angeles out front of this building with many of them coming to get their life right with Jesus Christ. He is bringing in the harvest."

"Amen to that Pastor," They reply simultaneously.

Pastor Timothy continues, "We must continually pray for wisdom. And let's make sure we keep this all about the cross of Christ, the blood He shed for us and the resurrected Savior. Let's keep it about denying ourselves and taking up our cross.[102] This is not about getting large homes and fancy suits. We are going to have to resist worldly possessions trying to come in to deceive us. Remember, *godliness is not a means to financial gain.*[103] Remember that Jesus Christ sent the Holy Spirit into the world to, *"convict the world of sin, and of righteousness, and of judgment"*[104] And then He placed His Spirit in us, so we are to allow Him to do the same through us. Many will be

---

[102] Matthew 16:24
[103] 1 Timothy 6:5 NLT
[104] John 16:8

saved because of Him working through us, but also, *"many will be offended,*[105]

"but blessed is he who is not offended because of Him." [106]

When Jeremiah was persecuted, he was tempted to stop his preaching but then he said,

"But His word was in my heart like a burning fire shut up in my bones; I was weary of holding it back, And I could not."[107]

John the revelator was thrown out on the island of Patmos because of the Word of God.[108] We are faced with a difficult task so let's keep alert and be willing to pay the price. We will need each other, now let's get out there and pray and worship with the others."

---

[105] Matthew 24:10
[106] Matthew 11:6

[107] Jeremiah 20:9
[108] Revelation 1:9

As they walk into the sanctuary from the back door that leads to the stage. They notice that the worship team is singing, and the place is full. Everybody in the building was seeking the Lord in prayer and crying out for forgiveness of sins. The glory of the Lord was being poured out in that building on all the people. As Johnnie looks across the sanctuary, he sees the young man who had his sight restored when Silas was praying for him the other day. The young man was wearing baggy pants with a couple holes in them and a shirt that seemed dirty and didn't fit right. It was apparent he has not been able to shower for some time. Johnnie's heart was filled with joy to see this young man falling in love with Jesus Christ.

As Johnnie begins to internally thank the Lord for this young man's healing, he is overcome with the Holy Spirit and falls to his knees in awe of the wonderful presence of Jesus Christ.

After a few hours of prayer and worship Johnnie approaches this young man and says, "Hi, my name is Johnnie, I'm so excited to see all that the Lord Jesus has done for you. What is your name?"

"My name is James, and I have never experienced anything like this in my life. I was born into a gang, raised with a 9mm in my hands. I have been doing drugs since I was six years old and got stabbed in the eye when I was twelve. My parents told me I was a tough kid. And that they were proud of the way that I handled myself on the streets. But a kid named Steven invited me to the service the other day, and for some weird reason I came. And I don't want to be tough anymore. I am now fourteen years old and I never want to go home again. I hope to serve Jesus Christ. He is so real to me now."

"Well James," said Johnnie, "I know Steven, he is a good friend, and I can see that you have been born again James. And if you don't want to go home to a gang atmosphere, we will do whatever we can to help you okay. We love you James and welcome you into the family of God. Let me, Silas, Steven or the Pastor know if you're hungry or if you need anything okay. That is what we are here for James. Do you have any friends here with you James?" Johnnie asks.

"No, I don't. I have just been coming alone, I love it here Johnnie. It is the most peaceful place that I have been."

"I agree says Johnnie."

Priscilla comes and introduces herself to James and gives him a hug and says, "Jesus Christ has you safe now James, *He will never leave you nor forsake you!*[109] Isn't He good."

"Yes mam," replies James. James looks at Johnnie and asks, "Man can I crash here tonight?"

---

[109] Hebrews 13:5

"You know James I was hoping you would ask, why don't you hang out with Steven, Silas and I so we can do some bible studies together and grow and mature in our relationship with Jesus together."

"That sounds great said James, thank you so much."

"Your welcome James, get with me a little later okay."

"Alright man, will do, I'm just going to stay right here and pray some more."

Johnnie and Priscilla walk away. They are filled with compassion for James due to all he had to go through prior to coming to knowing the presence and mercy of Jesus Christ.

"My goodness," says Priscilla, "What a sad story."

"Yes, it is Priscilla, but what a wonderful ending. Hallelujah!" Johnnie says with a look of amazement and joy in abundance on his face. He looks at Priscilla and says,

"*we rejoice with joy inexpressible and full of glory,*[110]

"I'm so glad you're fighting the good fight of faith with me Priscilla."

"Me too Johnnie, I cannot imagine living without Jesus Christ in my life."

"Me neither Priscilla, me neither. I'm going to go crash Priscilla. We are going to do some outreach tomorrow if you want to go you are welcome. Pray about it and let us know okay."

"Okay Johnnie, I will call you tomorrow. I am going to stay down here for a couple more hours and pray with some people. Have a good night."

---

[110] 1 Peter 1:8

178

Chapter 9

Seeking to Save the Lost

The next morning Johnnie awakes and hurries to the prayer room to meet with Silas and Steven to pray for direction for today's evangelistic efforts. Steven walks in and says, "I got the coffee, where is Silas?"

"I don't know man. I haven't seen him this morning, I'm sure he'll be here soon." replies Johnnie. "I was talking to Priscilla last night and she might go out with us today."

"Oh, cool." says Steven, "The more the merrier." Johnnie and Steven open their bibles when Silas and Priscilla walk in.

"Hey, good morning Priscilla, Silas. Did you all get a good night's sleep?"

"No, replies Silas with a grin, I went to bed about an hour ago."

"Ha, me too." Replies Priscilla. "Hey you guys. I was talking to James last night and he really wants to go with us today on the streets. He said he wants to see more people experience the love of God as he has. I told him I would talk to you about it and let him know. What do you think?" Asks Priscilla.

"I think it would be awesome," they all replied.

"Great, i'll go get him." Says Priscilla, "I'll be right back," as she darts out the door.

Priscilla quickly returns with James and they all start to pray and seek the Lord's direction for the day.

As they were praying Steven says, "Why don't we all write down where we want to go today and put the papers on the table. And then before we head out we can read them?"

"Okay" says Silas, "Good idea"

After an hour of prayer Johnnie opens the papers they had written on. Every one of them says, 'Compton.'

"Alright you guys, looks like we're going to Compton."

"Whoo hoo," replies Priscilla, "God is going to seek and save the lost today."

They jumped in the church van and headed toward their destination.

James says, "Hey you guys, thanks for letting me come. To be honest I am a little nervous about witnessing to people. I'm not sure what to say to them."

"Don't even worry about it James," replies Silas. "You don't have to say anything if you don't want to. Just come and hang out with us. And if the Lord puts it on your heart to share your testimony with someone than just do the best you can. The Lord will use you right where you're at, we are free."

"I never know what I am going to say," replies Johnnie. "I usually just read the bible as much as I can and as I talk to people that is what comes out of my mouth. So dont worry about it. If you want to, you can just be praying for everyone while we are out there."

"Okay," says James.

Upon arriving at their destination, they park the van in a local grocery store parking lot. Then begin to walk through the neighborhood.

"Man, I can sure feel the Holy Spirit out here with us." Says Priscilla.

"Yeah so can I." said Johnnie.

Walking along Priscilla sees a home with the front door open. The house has steel bars on all the windows and a Pitbull tied up to a large tree in the front yard. There are two empty bottles of wine labeled, *mad dog 20-20* laying in the front yard. The yard is mostly dirt with little patches of grass that could use some water. They all notice that there is a lot of yelling and screaming going on from inside the house. They also notice a little boy crying and wearing only a diaper as he rides his little tricycle along the side of the house. Priscilla is instantly filled with the Holy Spirit and the gift of faith. She is overcome with compassion for this little boy's living situation. She says to the group, "Hey look, the gate is open. That means we have a full invitation to go and talk with these people."

"I don't know if that's a good idea, that could be dangerous. They don't sound like they are in a real good mood." Says James.

Priscilla looks at Johnnie and whispers, "Nothing is stopping me from bringing the love of God to this home. And I do not expect anyone to go with me, but fear is not going to stop me."

Johnnie gets a huge grin and says, "I love you Priscilla, let's go."

As Johnnie and Priscilla walk on to the property the Pitbull starts to bark uncontrollably as he lunges toward them violently showing his teeth.

James says with fear in his voice, "I am praying that his chain doesn't break. Staring at the large Pitbull trembling with fear. Next thing they know there is a large man with a bottle of wine in his hand at the door. James is thinking, "He must weigh 260 pounds!"

He is wearing a white tank top, dark sunglasses, and a black bandana around his head while being totally covered with tattoos. With his eyebrows tipped downward and a gruff voice he says, "What are you kids doing here? Get the hell out of here."

"Sir, we have come to tell you that Jesus Christ loves you. He has been pouring out His Spirit at our church and healing a lot of people. We would love the opportunity to come and pray with you guys and share His message of hope with you." Priscilla said with much conviction.

The man replied, "Get the hell out of here you little tramp."

"Sir please, we are here to share with you the message of Jesus Christ and to offer you and your family His hope."

After hearing him call her a tramp the man's wife comes out and hits her husband on the forehead with a frying pan. The man leans downward placing his hands on his face. With blood dripping on the concrete stairway he leans up and she goes to strike him again. His wife sees the blood and refrains from hitting him again.

As they continue arguing even more Johnnie walks up toward them and pleads boldly, "Please stop fighting. We are here to talk with you both right now. Now stop it, in the name of Jesus Christ."

Meanwhile Silas is holding the little boy who was riding his tricycle. Trying to keep the little boy from seeing all the violence and stop him from crying.

Priscilla notices that the little boy is crying and has a runny nose as Silas holds him. She is filled with compassion. Fear has no hold on her as she says, "You two, we are not leaving unless you give us thirty minutes to tell you about Jesus Christ and His message of hope. And if you do not want to listen, I will stay right here and bug you all day long. Now please, let's go in and sit down. It won't take long."

James is thinking, "This girl is crazy!" James is still standing in the safety of the front gate wondering if they are even going to make it back to the church or not.

Meanwhile Priscilla, staring at these people with eyes expressing hope, love, compassion, strength and obviously not willing to back off.

The man's eyes are open as he sees her passionate expression. As if he can now see that these kids really are sincere. He looks at

186

Priscilla and says, "I am sorry mam, please forgive me."

"That's right your sorry, you big jerk, now let's give these kids a chance and listen to what they have to say." Said the man's wife.

As they enter the home James seems to feel safer staying closer to the front door. Johnnie is noticing that James seems a little nervous. He gives James a grin, winks at him with confidence to hopefully help him relax a bit.

Steven starts out saying, "Hey you two we really appreciate you allowing us to come into your home."

"Well, we really didn't have a choice did we?" Says the large man as he is wiping blood off his forehead.

"Be nice Bernard or I'll give you another bump on the other side of your forehead." Says his wife. Priscilla trying not to giggle at the mans wife's statement says, "Sorry for being so bold in our approach this morning but I really feel like God wants to give you both a fresh start in life. He wants to fill your hearts with His love. I'd like to introduce you two to our friend James who recently became a Christian. James, why don't you share with Bernard and his wife what God did for you at church the other day?"

James looking nervous began saying, "Well, to be honest I was raised on these streets right here, and up until a few days ago I was getting high and selling drugs. I was stabbed in my right eye and lost sight when I was younger fighting on these streets. And then one day just last week Steven came and invited me to church. I was thinking, who is this crazy white guy, and why am I even considering going to church with him? But when I walked into church. I could literally experience the presence, and love of Jesus Christ. I repented of my sins and as we were praying the Lord healed my eye and I can see again. But even more importantly than that, He filled my heart with love, joy, and peace."

Steven interrupts and says, "I literally watched as the Lord healed his eye. It was gray when we began to pray, when instantly it turned the same color brown as the other one."

Priscilla steps in and says, "Ya know the Bible says that,"

"Behold, now is the accepted time; behold, now is the day of salvation."[111]

While Priscilla was speaking this. The Holy Spirit filled the home with His presence and Bernard began to get teary eyed and said, "You know, I was raised in the south, and was brought up in a good Christian home. I went off to serve in the military and came to Los Angeles where I met my wife. I have never really been back to church or felt like the same person since I have gotten back from war. I am sitting here drinking at 11:00 am in the morning. I am not a real good husband and I feel like a horrible father to my

---

[111] 2 Corinthians 6:2

young son Isaac. I hate the life I am living. Do you suppose there is still hope for me?"

Johnnie steps in and says, "Bernard, there is hope for you. But it is not in any religious type of system. It is only in Jesus Christ."

Bernard looks at his wife and says, "Shania baby, I love you, and I want to be a better husband and father. Please forgive me. I am going to start going to church with these kids and ask God to help me be a better man."

As tears begin to stream down Shania's face she says, "Oh baby, I know you do, and I'm sorry I hit you upside your head with that pan.

Bernard grabs little Isaac and holds him close as he starts to cry aloud. Shania went over and held her husband. They were filled with forgiveness and love. There is not a dry eye in the room as the Holy Spirit is poured out on Bernard, Shania, and little Isaac.

Priscilla whispers to Johnnie radiating in awe and full of excitement. "There was not even a prayer or nothing. And God filled them with His Spirit."

Bernard hands little Isaac to Shania and began to gather the booze and drug paraphernalia throughout the house and carries it out front to the trash cans. He was crying out saying, "Get the hell out of my life alcohol. Don't ever come back. I am living for Jesus now."

Shania is kneeling on the floor experiencing the love of God and embracing little Isaac. She is so overcome with love she can barely speak. Bernard comes back in and grabs little Isaac again and they were all sitting on the floor rejoicing over all that the Lord was doing for their family.

Johnnie decided it would be best for the Holy Spirit to finish what He came to do and left a Bible and a church flyer on the table with his phone number on it. Conversation was no longer needed at this point. Bernard's family was experiencing the new birth in the power and love of the Holy Spirit.

They were heading back toward the van in amazement and awe, smiling from ear to ear.

Johnnie says,

"For God had made them rejoice with great joy![112]

Upon approaching the parking lot where the church van is parked. They noticed a group of seven gang members looking in their direction. They see the van has spray paint on it that says, *"Go home!"* The gang members start to cuss at Johnnie and the team saying, "Your all not welcome here. If you come back, we will pop a cap in you."

As one of the gang members says, "Hey James, is that you? Did you join that stupid church holms? You better be careful around here

---

[112] Nehemiah 12:43

homey. We don't need any of that religion in our hood."

Silas tells the group to just get in the van and ignore them. Johnnie says, "Yeah I think that is a good idea, let's go you guys."

As they are driving back to the church James opens his bible and reads for a second. Then he says with a lot of excitement, "Hey look you guys this is so cool. This is what my bible just fell open to,

"For I determined not to know anything among you except Jesus Christ and Him crucified. I was with you in weakness, in fear, and in much trembling. And my speech and my preaching were not with persuasive words of human wisdom, but in demonstration of the Spirit and of power, that your faith should not be in the wisdom of men but in the power of God." [113]

---

[113] 1 Corinthians 2:2-5

"Man, that is awesome. That is definitely true for us today. Our speech, when we were witnessing to that family was not full of human wisdom. But the power of God showed up and impacted their life. I am so excited for them. I just know we will be seeing them in church soon." Said James. "Oh, and by the way. Who is going to explain to Pastor Timothy his new church van has nice new paint on it that says, *Go home?*"

They all began laughing and praising God as they drove back to the church.

Chapter 10
Persecution Begins

Arriving back at the church the Pastor called the five of them into his office. Pastor Timothy began saying, "Hey you guys, I was in prayer feeling overwhelmed regarding what we are going to do as far as feeding and helping all these new converts. When I heard the Holy Spirit ask me, *"why not go purchase the abandoned hotel across the street?"* I answered, "But Lord, how can we do this if we don't have the money?" The Lord replied,

Do you not yet understand, or remember the five loaves of the five thousand and how many baskets you took up? Nor the seven loaves of the four thousand and how many large baskets you took up?[114]

---

[114] Matthew 16:9-10

He continued saying, *"Do you believe that with the Lord all things are possible?"*

I responded, "Yes Lord, I do believe."

Pastor continued sharing, "After this I sat in my chair and my phone rang. I picked it up and a Pastor from a large church in Texas had heard what is going on out here and said that the Lord had put it on his congregations' heart to help us financially. To add some building space if needed. I told him that I was looking at an abandoned building just across the street from our church and that it would be perfect for housing new converts. And putting them through a discipleship program. He told me they will be researching the property online and contacting them to purchase that building for us. He also told me they will begin to fund raise to help us put some money in it. They promised not to stop until they earned a million dollars that we could put into the building and build a sanctuary in it.

Priscilla's eyes are filled with tears of joy on hearing this news. They were all overcome with amazement in the presence and power and love of almighty God.

Pastor being led by the Holy Spirit. Walks over to James and places his hand on his shoulder and says, "James, you have been abandoned by people in this life, but the Lord says, you will never be abandoned by Him. You are going to be doing daily Bible studies with new Christians and heading up a mentoring program.

"But Pastor, I'm a brand-new Christian myself, how can this be?"

"James, you will have some time to prepare. "But the Lord has spoken clearly to me on this issue and He wants you to know that you have a significant role to play in this ministry. You are a new creation. The past is behind you, and you need to start seeing yourself as loved and with a purpose. God is raising you up young man."

"Wow Pastor, I'm overwhelmed." James says as he has a hard time standing feeling overwhelmed with gratitude for all that the Lord has done for him. With tears of joy streaming down his face in the presence of God, James cries out, "Why me Lord? I don't deserve this. I will do the best I can for you Jesus, I will do the best I can."

"Hey Pastor, do you think it would be okay to use some of that money for a couple of buses that we could use for the outreach?" Asks Johnnie.

"I think that's a great idea Johnnie. Tomorrow we will all go take a walk around the building and get some ideas together. Man, I feel like a kid again," said Pastor. "This is exciting."

The next day they are all excited to go see what the Lord had given to them. After some time in prayer and bible study they ate some breakfast and headed across the street to walk around the building.

"Man Pastor, this hotel has five stories and three wings. This thing is huge." Says Silas.

Pastor Tim replied, "I'm thinking we could use the bottom floor and 1st floor for classrooms and educational purposes. And use the other four floors for housing. There's plenty of parking."

Priscilla says, "I wonder what they are going to do with those hotel vans over there? I'm thinking those may be included in the price of the building."

Steven asks, "But where are we going to put the sanctuary?"

"I don't know, maybe we will have to just enlarge the one we're using and make a good crosswalk across the street. We do have room to enlarge it." Said Pastor Tim.

After walking around the building, they come to the corner to cross the street heading back to the church. Suddenly an old Chevy Impala with flashy green paint speedily pulls up into the parking lot they were in. Four gang members came pouring out of the passenger seat. The female driver stayed behind the wheel keeping the car running. With loud Rap music blaring from the car. The four gang members approach Pastor Tim and the group. Steven saw that the gang member has a gun tucked in the front of his pants with the handle showing.

The lead gang member warned them sternly saying, "I told you all you are not welcome in our hood. Ya'll are messing with our business. Do you think that paint on your van is the worst thing that we will do to you? Everybody in this town is getting religious because of ya'll. We are not going to allow that to happen."

Steven full of the Spirit steps forward and says, *"Who are you to come against the army of the Lord? We will proclaim this gospel in this neighborhood and His Word will go forth in power!*

At this, the lead gang member is furious, and with his eyebrows tipped in anger. He steps forward toward Steven and says, "Oh yeah, around here they call me Pockets. And you're about to learn not to talk to me with no respect. Pockets whips out his pistol and quickly aims it at Steven and shoots him right in the chest. With the loud deafening sound of the gun shot, and the smell of smoking gun powder lingering in the air. Steven is thrown back and falls to the ground from the impact. Instantly everything suddenly seems to be at a standstill. A surreal moment of disbelief hits Pastor Tim and the others. It is as if everything is silent and blurry.

Pockets and the gang members run back to the car and dive in. The female driver squeals the tires as they quickly drive away leaving tire smoke, gun smoke and blood in their midst.

With the smell of gun powder and burnt rubber from the car tires spinning. Steven lays bleeding on the ground. Priscilla lets out a loud scream as Pastor Tim calls 911. Johnnie quickly leans over Steven and says frantically, "It's going to be okay Steven, just stay with us buddy." With tears streaming down his face. Silas is also bent over Steven crying uncontrollably.

Steven says softly, *"Father, forgive them for they know not what they do,"* he looks at Johnnie and softly says, "It's okay Johnnie, it's okay," barely having the strength to speak.

With 911 dispatched Pastor Tim, Priscilla, Johnnie, and Silas are all kneeling around Steven quietly praying and encouraging Steven.

Suddenly Steven sees a bright glorious light come down from heaven. There was also a cloud of saints who have gone on before him cheering him on. Steven is in a lot of pain, but Pastor Tim notices Steven begins to smile and softly whispers, "You guys, stop crying it's okay, can't you see it? Can't you see it? It's beautiful, wonderful. As he can barely get the words out due to the pain he is experiencing.

Priscilla says, "Just hold on Steven, I can hear the ambulance now. Just hang on, please Steven."

Steven barely gets these words out, "Don't let anything stop you guys from going into that neighborhood. For even now, we have the victory in Christ Jesus our Lord." [115]As his eyes close and he breathes his last breath.

Everything happened so fast the group is in unbelief. In total shock and speechlessness as they kneel around Stevens lifeless body. The paramedics and police arrive insisting they move back from Steven so they can try to revive him. The police begin to question them to find out who did this.

The paramedics did not even try long to revive Steven. They quickly placed a white sheet over Stevens body and began their investigation before they took Stevens body away. The police

---

[115] 1 Corinthians 15:57

did receive a description of the getaway car, gang members and pockets street name. The group stood in disbelief until finally there was nothing else to do. Except walk back over to the church.

Meanwhile Steven is being taken toward this light by angels. Thousands of people rejoicing being exceedingly excited to see him. Steven sees the Lord, and notices His eyes are full of love. Steven knows Jesus is excited to show Steven all He has for him.[116] And then, the Lord said to him,

"Well done, good and faithful servant; you have been faithful over a few things, I will make you ruler over many things. Enter into the joy of your lord.' Matt 25:23

The End....

---

[116] Luke 12:32

Please read an especially important note from the author on the next page.

A Note from the Author

I want to make a public proclamation that this story is fiction. And that God's Holy Bible is the ONLY infallible written Truth that we as Christians should use as our guide.

I also want to say that all true missionary and evangelistic outreach is birthed into Christians through their prayer life and obedience to God Almighty.

The bible gives no mentions of miracles, signs, and wonders in the ministry of John the Baptist. (And Jesus called him the greatest of prophets) And we as Christians should NOT make miracles a priority, our priority should be a pure, repentant, obedient heart unto our God.

Jesus told the towns people where he performed most of His miracles, *"Woe to you, Chorazin! Woe to you, Bethsaida! For if the miracles that were performed in you had been performed in Tyre and Sidon, they would have **repented** long ago in sackcloth and ashes.*

Matthew 11:21

Jesus finished that up to these people with these words, *"will you be lifted to the heavens? No, you will go down to hell."* Matthew 11:23

(you can receive a miracle, not repent, and still go to hell)

*Jesus said, "I tell you, there is **rejoicing** in the presence of the **angels** of God **over** one sinner who <u>**repents**</u>"*

Luke 15:10

The emphasis on all true ministry birthed from the Holy Spirit of God will always be on repentance, righteous living, and holiness. If miracles, signs and wonders come, Great! They are gifts from God, to His remnant, for His purpose, and it is exciting to see God move in mighty ways. And God has not removed the ministry of His Holy Spirit, nor will He! He promised them to us, and never will He forsake us!

Jesus said, *"Nevertheless do not rejoice in this, that the spirits are subject to you, but rather rejoice because your names are written in heaven."* Luke 10:20

Is your name in that book? If so, are you obeying Jesus in the great commission? *"Selah"*

Michael Stokes

Blessings,,,,,,,,,,, Romans 15:13

Apostles Creed

Michael Stokes

Made in the USA
Columbia, SC
05 February 2024

31445345R00124